LOVE FOR THE SPINSTER

Also by Kasey Stockton

Women of Worth Series
Love in the Bargain
Love at the House Party
Love in the Wager
Love in the Ballroom

Ladies of Devon Series
The Jewels of Halstead Manor
The Lady of Larkspur Vale

Stand Alone Regency Romance
His Amiable Bride
A Duke for Lady Eve
A Forgiving Heart

Contemporary Romance
Snowflake Wishes
His Stand-in Holiday Girlfriend
Snowed In on Main Street

LOVE
for the Spinster

WOMEN OF *Worth* BOOK TWO

KASEY STOCKTON

Golden Owl Press

This is a work of fiction. Names, characters, places, and incidents either are the product of the author's imagination or are used fictitiously. Any resemblance to actual persons, living or dead, events, or locales is entirely coincidental.

Copyright © 2019 by Kasey Stockton
Cover design by Once Upon a Cover

First print edition: June 2019
All rights reserved. No part of this book may be reproduced or used in any manner without written permission of the copyright owner except for the use of quotations for the purpose of a book review.

*For Granny, who gave me a love of history,
and Grandma, who gave me a love of reading.*

CHAPTER 1

This was it, the perfect opportunity. I crouched low behind the sofa and eyed my opposition sunning in the window as though he held no cares in the world—which, in truth, he didn't. His eyes closed lazily and his body slouched against the seat cushions in contented rest, his long tail sliding along the window panes.

Tiptoeing from my hiding place, I gripped the blanket in my fingers, inching closer to the orange tabby. He stilled as though he sensed what was coming. I leapt, closing the blanket around the petulant cat and pulling him from the windowsill in one quick motion. Swiftly closing the edges of the blanket together, I held it at arm's length to avoid Jasper's sharp, swiping claws.

Skipping down the ornately carved staircase, I deposited the angry bundle in the drawing room before closing the door quickly behind me. My chest heaved with adrenaline, my back resting against the floral, painted door. Aunt Georgina might have had a penchant for strays when she was alive, but that didn't mean I had to put up with this one's cantankerous attitude infiltrating my personal space—even though I could never find it in me to rid the house of him altogether. But regardless, the pink sitting room was exactly that: mine.

My shoulders slouched. How very pompous of me. I was in this home as a guest. Aunt Georgina wasn't a direct relation of mine, but she was more like family than my real one had been in quite some time. In one sense it was a massive blessing to have been thrown at the mercy of Georgina Stewart, for I would never have obtained independence otherwise. But it did not keep me from carrying a heavy weight of anger toward the man who called himself my father—and neither did it lessen his deceit.

"You've a caller, Miss Hurst," Perkins, the butler said stiffly, his tall build framed by the small corridor. "Lady McGregor. And this came just now." He held out a tray, and I took the letter, my heart springing at the familiar scrawl. The aging steward over my country house, Corden Hall, delivered the most diverting anecdotes among his estate business, and I looked forward to his notes above anything else. They were the bright spot of my mostly placid days.

Blowing a lock of unruly, red hair away from my forehead, I glanced over my shoulder, jumping when Jasper scratched at the door from inside the room.

Clearing my throat, I clasped my hands before me, careful not to crease the letter. "I believe Jasper requires the drawing room at present, Perkins. Perhaps it would be prudent to give him time to cool off. Pray show her into the Pink Room."

"Very good." He bowed away, not bothering to hide his irritation. I officially took over as mistress when Aunt Georgina died, but I'd been running the place since she took me on as her companion, so the shift was natural.

Perkins was a newer addition to the household after Aunt Georgina's last butler retired. Stolen from another matron whom Aunt Georgina had never much liked, Perkins had always been loyal to her, and was never sour. But though he was never rude to me, not precisely, I could tell from the beginning he did not care for me. I had yet to solve precisely what I had done to earn his disfavor, but I had a strong inclination that my parentage was to blame.

Even members of the lower classes looked down on the illegitimate.

Lifting my jade green skirts, I climbed the stairs to the Pink Room, reveling in the absence of felines within my sanctuary. The mauve curtains were pulled away from the window, gathered with golden cord and allowing the bright noon sun to pour into the room and warm the space. I tucked the letter in the top drawer of my writing table to be enjoyed later.

Rosalynn swept into the room, her protruding belly not hampering in any way her ability to sashay with the greatest dignity and poise. "Good day, darling," she purred.

I swallowed a chuckle as she settled herself into the deep plum padded chair, arranging her skirts over her knees and then training her dark brown gaze on me. I found, as I often did in Rosalynn's presence, that I was certain I was doing something very wrong when she looked at me in such a manner. Logically, I was aware I was not breaking any etiquette or committing a social *faux pas*, but her piercing gaze had the ability to make me question my every move regardless. It always had.

"You are in the family way?" I confirmed, unsure of whether I was meant to know that already or not. It was hard to keep track with Rosalynn, and I had not seen her in quite some time.

"Yes, this will make five," she answered nonchalantly, waving her hand in disregard. She had the bearing of a countess and wore her title in the set of her shoulders and lift of her chin since marrying Lord McGregor. "Or six, if the pattern of twins is to be continued. The children have been begging for a visit from Aunt Freya, but I told them you are far too dull to travel."

I shrugged. It was perhaps not my favorite thing to travel the length of England simply to stay in Rosalynn's drafty castle with her brood of noisy children. Boys, all of them.

A catlike smile tipped her lips. "But I told Jack to leave it to me. I would bring you and the children together one way or another."

Apprehension filtered into my stomach. Rosalynn typically did not make threats she was incapable of upholding. She was the one who instigated The Sisterhood of Deserving Females in our school days and convinced Elsie and me to agree to never marry, thus giving our power over to another man. She could be very persuasive when she felt so inclined.

I was probably the most hesitant at the delicate age of twelve to agree to such a dramatic scheme, yet I was the only one of the three of us who remained unwed. A fact unlikely to ever change.

Brushing aside memories of our past, I delivered a bright smile. "Has Lord McGregor traveled with you to Town?"

"Yes, of course. The whole lot of them came."

"Then it would seem unnecessary for me to visit you at the castle, anyway." I offered her an impish grin. "That must have been a lively trip." She had been blessed with two sets of twins, and they were just over a year apart. I imagined the carriage ride across England with Rosalynn sitting in the very center and her four boys climbing about like cheerful little monkeys. She was poised in the center of it all, naturally.

Rosalynn cast her gaze up, chuckling. "I assure you I cannot endure it again any time soon. We shall be here for quite some time."

"And the baby?"

Her hand moved to her rounded midsection, as though subconsciously checking her child. Her dark eyes warmed and she spoke softly. "There are plenty of fine doctors in London."

Perkins held the door open while the maid carried in the tea service and set it on the table before me. She scurried back out the door, and it closed behind her with a thunk.

I prepared the tea and passed a steaming cup to Rosalynn.

"How are the cats?" she prodded, eyeing me from over the top of her tea cup, her dark eyebrow raised in question.

I speared her with a wry look. "Everywhere."

"You do know," she began slowly, "you are not required to keep them any longer. Now that Georgina…"

The room fell quiet, and I picked up a slice of shortbread, taking a bite and chewing the rich, buttery treat slowly while I formed my words. It was perhaps difficult for Rosalynn to comprehend, and I was unsure if I even needed to explain myself to her. She was, however, one of my very dearest friends. I was certain she simply wanted to understand. "It has been six months since Aunt Georgina's death, yes, and I have put off mourning clothes." I plucked at my green skirt as if that solidified my point. I had remained in black far longer than was necessary. "But I cannot so easily put off those wretched cats. This is her home, after all, and she adored the beastly things. Every single one of them."

"*Was* her home," she corrected.

"True, and now it belongs to Elsie."

"Does that bother you?" Rosalynn asked, never one to shy away from difficult questions.

I tucked my chin, shocked at her insinuation. "No, of course not. I may have been Aunt Georgina's companion for the last three years of her life, but Elsie was her great-niece. It was not my place to inherit the house."

Rosalynn's sharp eye remained fixed on me. "Many of us expected it, though."

"I did not," I said with a note of finality which I hoped rang clear. I was not left the house in Aunt Georgina's will, but I was left a sum of money that would keep me content for the rest of my days. Though, that was not public knowledge. I wasn't quite sure if even Elsie knew of it.

"I should invite you to dine," Rosalynn said, deftly altering the course of the conversation, "but we only arrived last evening, and I need a few days to get the house in order first. Shall we say Sunday?"

"That would be splendid," I lied. It had been a slow building occurrence, but ever since my father threw our family into scandal, I felt a certain level of discomfort in social settings. Not that we went out all that often. Most of the time people came to Aunt Georgina's home. But the setting seemed to matter very little, for I would find myself nervous and shaky in company, even in our own drawing room.

"We shall keep it small," Rosalynn said, "but I know Jack will love to see you."

A whimper sounded near the window, and I looked up sharply. I had thought Jasper was the last of the cats. He was certainly the most volatile. I listened to Rosalynn describe the changes she'd like to make to the townhouse Lord McGregor inherited with his title. Her mother-in-law had recently given over reign of the home to her and now, after three years of marriage, she had the ability to redecorate the outdated home however she wished.

Hot tea steamed from my cup, warming my fingers. I did my best to give my attention to Rosalynn but found my mind wandering to the letter awaiting me in my writing table.

A dark brown tail poked from behind a chair situated near the window and I found my face relaxing into a smile. Pursing my lips, I delivered a sharp whistle, effectively cutting Rosalynn off in the midst of describing a butter yellow wallpaper she had fallen in love with. Coco, the chocolate colored terrier, promptly jumped from her hiding spot and obediently came to sit by my feet. I scooped her up and carried her to the sofa, holding her scruffy, aging little body much like a baby.

"She is still around?" Rosalynn asked with no little surprise.

"She is a little lazier, but no less spunky for her age." I stroked her ears affectionately. I loved nothing in the world more than my sweet little dog.

"Do you remember the day we found her?" I asked.

"Yes, Elsie threw a fit when we left her behind at the park."

"And then your brother went back and searched for her. Did he know then that he was in love with Elsie?"

Rosalynn's eyebrows scrunched together in thought. "I doubt it. I wonder if he knew his feelings for quite some time."

I could understand that.

"Have you been busy these last few months?" she asked. "It is a little strange arriving to Town in the middle of the Season."

"I haven't been out much," I admitted, focusing on Coco's scruffy fur. I was yet unused to attending events without Aunt Georgina. "I'm only just out of mourning."

"We shall have to change that." She rose, smoothing her skirts around her perfectly round belly. Her cheeks positively glowing, she certainly wore motherhood well. "I can see myself out. I look forward to Sunday."

With a grin, she was off, and I slumped onto the sofa the moment the door closed behind her. Dropping my head back to rest on the sofa, I sighed. Coco lifted her head, tilting it to the side in support.

Had I not fully established myself as a spinster on the shelf so that I might be able to control my own social schedule? Less than one day back in London and Rosalynn was already throwing a rock into my perfectly developed plan. If I wasn't careful, I would soon be back to the innocent, obedient miss I was before I came to live with Aunt Georgina and learned the value of independence and self-government. The last four years had been a struggle and certainly had their ups and downs, but one clear benefit was how I had come into my own sense of self.

Now I simply had to figure out how to show that to Rosalynn.

CHAPTER 2

The McGregor townhouse was antiquated in its design, and all the more lavish for its old-fashioned decor. The rich burgundy and gold colors saturated the drawing room and created an aura of regal prestige. Why Rosalynn was planning on replacing it all with butter yellow wallpaper was beyond me—not that she would have trouble appearing refined and graceful in any setting.

The dinner party was small. I sat on a couch near the fireplace and listened politely as Lord McGregor's cousin, Mr. Kimble, droned on about his superior ability to tell at once if a person was lying to him. His jowls quivered with his endless chatter and I could not help but stare at the jiggly skin, my fingers tightening over each other in an effort to remain composed. Nodding solemnly, I sifted through my imagination for a suitable lie to test his abilities. If I was forced to converse with a stranger, I may as well have a little fun with it.

The door opened to admit another couple, and my fingers relaxed at once, watching the familiar eyes search the room until they landed on my own. My heart warmed as I took in Elsie's compassionate gaze, her arm leaving Lord Cameron's side as she sped across the floor to embrace me.

"This is a surprise," I said into her curled fringe as her tight embrace gripped me. She smelled much the same as she always had. Her coral gown set off her honey-colored hair to advantage, her comforting presence enfolding me like a thick, wool blanket. This was familiar; it was home.

"As I wanted it to be." She stepped back and raked her gaze over me in her assessing manner. It was clear from the first day our friendship formed that Rosalynn was in charge. Of the three of us she was indisputably the lead female. But Elsie had always had a sort of mothering relationship with me, stemming from her desire to shield me from Rosalynn's aggressive nature. Elsie probably didn't even realize that she had taken on the role of protector and mediator, but she was very much both of those things.

I sat on the vacated sofa. Mr. Kimble had gone away, though I did not know where to, and relief poured through me, my tense muscles relaxing. The man was a positive bore, but his attention made me anxious nonetheless.

Elsie sat beside me, picking up my hand in both of hers. I had the suspicion she was not planning on letting it go for some time.

"I did not realize you were back in England," I said.

"We've spent the last fortnight in Kent. It has been years since I've visited my parents."

"And how were you received?"

"Well enough." She shrugged, glancing to her husband laughing on the other side of the room with Lord McGregor. "Both my mother and father adore Cameron. It is I who chooses to spend as little time with them as possible."

"You've not forgiven them for lying to you during your Season?"

"I forgave them long ago," she said quickly. "I simply have

not forgotten. I find myself more at ease when I am not around them, 'tis all."

Elsie was a better person than I could ever dream to be. I had not yet forgiven my father for his misdeeds, and I doubted I ever would.

"Are you choosing to settle in Town?" I held my breath, hoping that would be the case.

She shook her head. "Not year-round. We have begun looking at estates to purchase. Cameron has tired of staying with relatives and wants a house for himself."

"But you travel so often."

She glanced away, a gleam in her eye betraying the emotion she was trying to hide. A tight smile stretched her lips to a thin line. "We do not plan to do that forever. It is time to settle down."

I opened my mouth to ask if there was a definitive reason for such a pronouncement—a baby, perhaps—but promptly closed it. I had made the mistake of inquiring about children years prior and discovered that Elsie was quite sensitive on the matter. Nearly four years of marriage without a baby had given enough tongues ammunition for wagging. I did not need to add mine to the list.

Rich smells wafted into the drawing room. Thick, beefy broths or perhaps a platter of pork must have been carried upstairs. My stomach rumbled accordingly.

"What shall you write about if not your exotic adventures?" I asked.

A small knowing smile graced her lips. "Perhaps we shall take a break from writing. Or perchance we will surprise everyone with a dull story based in London."

Disbelief lined my forehead. "You could not write dull."

"I don't write at all," she countered. "Cameron has that duty. I merely form the stories."

Laughing, I shook my head. "There is no 'merely' anything here. You have talent; accept it."

"And what have you been doing to fill your time?" She neatly changed the subject, tilting her head in avid interest. "I was so sorry we could not come to you when Aunt Georgina passed."

"We've managed. I thank you for your generosity in letting me stay on in the house. Oh!" I had a sudden thought, ignoring my rumbling stomach once again. "Would you like me to vacate it now that you are back?"

Her brows pulled together as she reclaimed her hand and set it in her lap. "Do not speak nonsense. I was hoping we could all stay there together. It is your home, though, Freya. Do not hesitate to tell me your true feelings on the matter."

There, speaking with Elsie, was the first time in years I'd held a conversation without the least bit of anxiety or alarm. I missed the comfort and warmth she exuded, and I found the prospect of spending time with her equal parts pleasant and relaxing. Besides, regardless of her sweet proclamations, the house was in fact hers, and I could never pretend otherwise. "I should like it above all things."

I speared Rosalynn with a glare. She sat regally at the foot of the table, a fork perched in her fingers as she smiled beatifically around the intimate dinner table. She either did not feel my vexation or chose to ignore it, but I was not going to let this go so easily. She had seated Mr. Kimble beside me, and if I was not much mistaken, she had done so as some sort of foolish matchmaking attempt.

"I do not feel it necessary to employ more than one housemaid," he said, his round nose twitching slightly. "And she has a sufficient amount of time to waste between her duties. I cannot fathom the expenditure for more than one." He took a swallow of his wine and shot me a triumphant grin. "She's got no one to chat with either, making her work efficient." He tapped his temple to indicate his superior line of thought.

I decided to test that superior brain in my own manner. "You are causing me panic, sir," I said with as much timidity as I could gather. "I've got three housemaids, you see, and I can only just imagine how often they must sit around chatting while there's work to be done."

He took a bite of his food and nodded. "They all do that."

"Maids?"

"Women."

I stiffened, my fork coming to a halt squarely above my boiled greens. Baring my teeth in the semblance of a smile, I kept my eyes on my plate. "Naturally."

"Natural, perhaps, but no less bothersome. This is what you need to do." He turned and his eyes locked on mine, revealing just how intensely he felt what he was saying. "You must release two of them."

His jowls were really quivering now.

"Oh, but I can't," I said with some surprise. "It is not my house. I am merely a guest."

"Then speak to the housekeeper. Ensure that the maids are all occupied in different areas of the house at all times. Avoid their crossing paths, too."

It was all I could do not to spray my bite of boiled greens all over the lovely table arrangement before me. I coughed down the food, chasing it with a drink. The flickering candlelight highlighted Rosalynn's arched eyebrow, and I smiled at her. So *now* she was interested.

"You have given me much to think on." I thanked Mr. Kimble gravely. The conversation had done nothing but prove that he was, in fact, a pompous toad and he did not have the ability, as he had previously claimed, to tell when a person was not being truthful. Not only did I feign interest, but my household did not have three housemaids. We had five. It was excessive by anyone's standards, but ours were not necessarily typical housemaids. One had sole responsibility over Aunt Georgina's animals, and another was in charge of the numerous plants.

Mr. Kimble spoke, pulling me from my musings. "Will you be attending the Fleming's ball on Friday next?"

"I don't believe so," I answered, wiping my mouth with a napkin.

"Drat, I had hoped to reserve a dance."

Dancing: one thing I sorely missed in recent years. Though, even if I were to attend the social Season, surely I was too old to dance with young, eligible males—I was off the market. Did Mr. Kimble not realize I had just turned three and twenty? I was a spinster, practically on the shelf. Not only had I obtained self-proclaimed independence, but my father had nailed the coffin closed on any chance of a reputable match when his marriage to my mother was revealed to be invalid, as he had already been married to a woman in France a few years prior. The secret family in his life turned out to be mine, and my mother and I had borne the brunt of his poor choices ever since. Gossip had cooled in the years since, in large part thanks to Aunt Georgina's patronage and the support of the regal Nichols family, but I would never be fully untainted again.

None of Society's basic acceptance of the cruel turn life had dealt me extended to the idea of matrimony, and I had reveled in the freedom from the marriage mart ever since. Not counting the odd man who was unaware of the gossip surrounding my name, Mr. Kimble among them.

He was simply going to have to be let down—and Rosalynn was going to have to be properly set down. I caught her gaze as she laughed at something her neighbor said, and she quirked a brow. My face was undoubtedly unpleasant, and she was going to learn she was the cause. It was unacceptable to try and matchmake me. I simply had to find a way to force her to see reason.

I rode home in Elsie's carriage that evening. The cab was quiet as we smoothly rumbled along. "How have you held up this year?" Lord Cameron inquired. His gaze was thoughtful. His arm rested around his wife, her head lolling on his shoulder.

"I have been well enough," I answered honestly. "I miss Aunt Georgina, of course."

"Naturally," he agreed. I couldn't help but think of Mr. Kimble and analyzed the differences between him and the kind man sitting across from me. How could Rosalynn possibly think that a man who complained of women talking too much would be an ideal fit for me? Four years ago, she would not have put up with any of that sort of talk in her presence, let alone at her own dinner table.

Though, to give her the benefit of the doubt, it was unlikely she had heard him spouting his nonsense from where she sat at the end of the table.

"I am glad you've come," I said.

"And I as well," he whispered. Soft snoring flowed from Elsie's unconscious form. Amusement colored his tone as he continued. "We've done quite a bit of traveling these last few weeks. She's plum worn out."

"Then hopefully she will sleep through the morning tomorrow."

Elsie slept through breakfast and then past noon. I began to wonder if we should send one of my numerous maids to check on her—they could idly be chatting if I did not find a good use for them—when she came into the pink sitting room and joined me for tea.

"Lord Cameron has gone to see his brother," I informed her when she seated herself on the settee beside me.

"Tarquin?" she asked, her eyebrows drawn together. "That's odd. They haven't been particularly close of late."

I filled a teacup and prepared it for Elsie, before requesting a plate of meats and cheeses. We drank tea while waiting for a heartier meal to be brought.

"I didn't know he was even in Town," she continued, setting her cup down. "He's acted oddly ever since the death of their brother. I know Cameron is concerned. I can only assume he decided to check in with Tarquin."

I shrugged. Another *useless* maid came in with a tray of food and set it on the table in front of our settee. I dismissed her so she would be free to chat excessively with the other incompetent maids and—

"Whatever is going on in your head?" Elsie asked, her honey-colored brows pulled together and a smile playing at her lips. "You look positively outraged."

I set my cup on the table, stretching my fingers to release the built-up tension. I hadn't been aware I was squeezing them so tightly. It was a blessing I had not shattered the cup.

"Freya?" she prompted.

"Rosalynn played matchmaker last evening."

Her head reared back slightly. "I thought you weren't interested in marriage. Have you changed your mind?"

I looked at her clearly, portraying my feelings as honestly as I knew how. "No. I still have zero desire to wed."

"Then perhaps you've misunderstood her intent?"

"No, it was apparent." I shook my head, Mr. Kimble's arrogant smile replaying in my mind. "And he was an overbearing, boastful idiot."

"What a review." Her eyebrows hitched higher on her forehead and then lowered again as if she considered my words. "I am sorry she did that to you."

"Time has blinded her," I said bitterly, my stomach souring from Rosalynn's betrayal.

Elsie picked up a plate and piled it with sliced ham and cheese, pulling a hunk of bread from the platter and dropping it on her plate. She speared me with a knowing glare from which I could not escape. "Or perhaps love has."

I could not control the scoff that burst forth. "Blinded her? *Love*?"

"Yes." Elsie chuckled, always the peacemaker. "Rosalynn is happy. I am sure she only wants you to feel that same happiness."

"I am happy," I defended.

"Of course you are." Elsie did not sound, even slightly, like she thought what she said was true.

"I *am*." It *was* true. I was content in the life I led. I had a comfortable home, friends who cared for me, and my steward's regular letters to keep me entertained. What more did I need?

We sipped our tea quietly as Lord Cameron entered the room and saved us from continuing that conversation. He took a seat on the chair beside his wife and reached over to hold her hand.

"How is Tarquin?" she asked.

Lord Cameron shook his head. "Didn't get to see him. He was busy."

"I didn't realize you were even going to try."

He glanced at her sharply, his mind turning. "I did not want to worry you. But alas, I shall have to try another time." He lowered his voice. "I do wonder if he is only avoiding me."

Elsie widened her eyes in such a way that spoke volumes of the argument they were silently carrying on and how often they had discussed this very thing. She speared him with a look before turning back to me. "Tell me about the cats," she said, a smile forcing her lips thin. There was a significant amount of information I was missing about Tarquin, it would seem, but now was not the proper time to fill in those gaps.

"Aunt Georgina could not say no," I said instead, pouring Lord Cameron a cup of tea. "She always blamed Coco, you know. After you brought the dog here, she discovered her love for animals. It was a slow accruement over the years, but she ended up with six cats and one dog."

"Six?" Lord Cameron expostulated.

I nodded, sipping my tea. "It is not so bad, really. Most of them keep to themselves. There's one little obnoxious tyrant, but since I've given him the drawing room he seems to be satisfied."

I caught the tail end of Elsie and Lord Cameron exchanging glances. It was hard not to feel a thread of resentment at their unified *understanding*. Of course six cats sounded excessive—it felt that way sometimes, too. But we did not gain six cats and a dog overnight. Aunt Georgina and I had proper time to acclimate to each additional animal. It was a slow progression in our household that outsiders did not quite understand.

There were many, many things outsiders did not understand, and I missed Aunt Georgina immensely as those things were brought to the forefront of my thoughts.

Elsie looked about her, sighing. "I have to admit that it feels strange to be in this house without Aunt Georgina. I find myself waiting to see her around corners or seated in her golden armchair."

Lord Cameron reached toward his wife again and took her hand, and I found myself averting my eyes. It was not so very forward or wrong of them, but it made me uncomfortable, though I knew not why.

Clearing my throat delicately, I pasted a smile on my face. "Are you planning to attend the Season while you are here?"

"Yes!" Elsie said, regaining her composure. "I've missed London parties. The people in part, but the dancing most of all."

"You did not dance in India?"

"We did," she said, a grin showing her teeth. "Though it was not quite the same. You shall have to wait for *The Golden Prince* to print and read all about it."

"Very well," I said with a nod. "I believe the Flemings are hosting a ball next week, but we have not received invitations to anything sooner."

"That suits me," Elsie said, chewing on a hunk of bread. "I should like to rest for a week at least, and then never leave England again. If you'll have us, that is."

I ignored her indication that she was the guest in this home. "I find I like your plan excessively. Now, if you'll excuse me, I just recalled that I have some correspondence from my steward I've yet to reply to."

"You have a steward?" Lord Cameron asked. "Does he take direction well?"

He forgot to add *from a woman*. It was true that men did not generally answer to women easily. Mr. Bryce was the exception, however. It was only a year earlier that he had replaced the aging steward my father had employed at the time of my inheritance over twenty years prior. I found Mr. Bryce through my man of business in London and we corresponded every fortnight, at least. Mr. Bryce kept me significantly more informed than his predecessor, and I found my interest in the people and happenings of Corden Hall growing with each missive. I'd done my best to match his stories wit for wit but as I lacked significant exposure in recent months to much society, my reservoir of interesting conversation pieces had run dry, and I was forced to resort to my antics with the cats.

I was walking a dangerous line with Mr. Bryce. As our communication grew more familiar, I found myself pretending I was communicating with a father figure—the type of man I wished mine was. Mr. Bryce mentioned my visiting Corden Hall in his last two letters and while the idea tempted me significantly—to say nothing of my desire to see the house and lands I owned—I was worried meeting the man would ruin the fantasy I was beginning to build in my head.

I faced Lord Cameron with my hands clasped before me. "He is actually quite agreeable. To say nothing of our recent increase in profits and gratifying reports on last year's harvest. I hope I never lose him."

CHAPTER 3

The Flemings had invited nearly everyone in London to their ball, and it seemed every single person had accepted. In my recent recession from polite society I had come to forget the mass amounts of people that would gather together in a ballroom and the resulting heat and stench. Anxiety gripped my spine as I was pushed from one group of women to the next, following Elsie in her rounds. She had not seen most of these people in years and had, apparently, quite a few to greet.

Not that I was surprised. Elsie and her husband became quite the sensation after their books began publishing. I knew her mother-in-law was not pleased with their writing career, but the majority of Society viewed it as an interesting oddity, and the couple was widely accepted.

Elsie had always been the friendly sort and conversed with ease. I used to be much the same way in my younger years. Recently, I couldn't claim the desire or the skill.

"But the last novel you put out was so romantic," the white-haired matron said, her ostrich feather bouncing along with her enthusiastic words. "I read the whole thing in one sitting, I vow."

"Thank you, Mrs. Doolittle." Elsie's sweet smile and no-nonsense expression clearly conveyed her genuine gratitude. "I appreciate the praise. I'm glad I could formulate such a gripping story for you."

Mrs. Doolittle preened, her ostrich feathers bouncing again as she dipped her aging head.

The strains of a waltz began, and Elsie jerked her head up. "I promised this dance to my husband. I should probably make myself easier to find."

Mrs. Doolittle shooed us away. Elsie dragged me toward the edge of the crowd and the opening of the dance floor. "I am going to find the ladies' retiring room," I said over the noise of music and chatter.

"No, you must dance!" Elsie complained, holding my hands in hers. "You said yourself it has been years, and I recall how much you used to enjoy it."

"The key words being *used to*," I said wryly.

"Oh, don't be such a spoilsport."

Mr. Kimble appeared by my side, and I startled at his sudden nearness. His shirt owned such high collar points his head could not move very far from side to side. I imagined the shirt point stabbing his long cheek the moment he turned sharply one way or the other. His smile, however, was uninhibited by the dangerous clothing, and he turned it on me with full force. "What a pleasant surprise to find you here, Miss Hurst. Would you like to dance?"

His dark coat and neatly arranged hair had him looking quite the gentleman—if a hound could look like a gentleman. I could almost forget his obnoxious conversation at dinner.

And I did so love dancing . . .

"Very well," I agreed, placing my hand on Mr. Kimble's impeccable sleeve and following him onto the dance floor. My breath caught in my throat as he swept me into the waltz. The heady feeling of floating around a waxed ballroom floor in the dim, warm lighting was making me dizzy, in an enjoyable way.

I had missed this.

"You are gifted," he said, guiding me around the set on lighter feet than I'd expected.

"Thank you, sir." I hated the way my voice sounded breathless and airy. I tried to filter more steadiness into my tone. "I have always had a special love for dancing."

"Yet you are not often found on the floor. Is there a reasonable explanation?"

I pursed my lips, wondering if my proclaimed illegitimacy was explanation enough for him.

I shrugged. The center of a ball was not exactly the ideal moment to bring up old scandals, particularly when they were better left forgotten.

Mr. Kimble slowed, his gaze narrowing in behind me. "What is that?"

The rest of the dancers continued to move, and I pulled Mr. Kimble along so we would not ruin the set. I glanced over my shoulder where the majority of the spectators' gazes were fixed, but I could not see over the crowds lining the room.

The din in the ballroom grew louder with gossip as we spun in graceful circles. There was some sort of event taking place and we were sure to hear of it the moment our dance ended.

"Perhaps it is Lady Melbourne," he continued, craning his neck as we danced. I tamped down my irritation; if Mr. Kimble wanted to act like an old gossip then that was his prerogative. Perhaps he was a true hunter, but instead of assisting with pheasants, his objective was gossip.

The final strains of the waltz came to a close, and I curtseyed to my distracted partner while he eyed the crowd near the doorway.

He did not bow, but instead said, "Lady Melbourne was seen

at Almack's last week throwing a cup of punch in a footman's face because he would not fetch her something stronger."

"Oh?" I placed my hand on his arm as he led me from the dance floor.

"And she gave Mrs. Folsom the cut direct at *her own* ball last month because she let her daughters wear dark colored gowns to their ball."

That was certainly rude of the woman. I had heard some of Lady Melbourne's antics in recent conversations, but never paid them any mind. She sounded, to me, an uptight, volatile woman, and I was glad not to run in the same circles as her. I was sure to receive the cut direct as well for my own claim to scandal, however long ago it occurred. People like that did not tend to forget blunders.

But still, what business of hers was it that the young women were wearing dark colors? "Are they debutantes?"

"No, but only recently out of the schoolroom. They both came out last Season."

In that case, the young women should have been dressed in pale colors to signify their innocence. I had never been one to care much about Society's standards, but many people did.

Lady Melbourne, evidently, was one of them.

We made it to the edge of the ballroom, and I was about to tell Mr. Kimble to leave me there as I was acting as my own chaperone, when we passed Lady Melbourne in quiet discussion with another woman.

"Not her, then," Mr. Kimble said, directing me further away. He seemed disappointed; another strike against him.

"We shall know soon enough," I remarked. Secrets had a way of making their way around a ballroom quicker than wheat on fire.

"I should think—" Mr. Kimble's words died on his lips as his eyes widened in synchronized fashion with his mouth. I glanced over my shoulder in the direction he was staring and found my own face falling slack.

I could not believe what I was seeing.

The crowd seemed to part like the Red Sea for Moses and a man stepped from the throng, his fancy clothing and exquisitely styled hair no match for the splendor and magnificence adorning the woman beside him. They reeked of money and prestige, and the smug looks on their faces revealed their prideful self-satisfaction.

"Is that—"

"Yes," I said, swallowing a lump, unable to shift my gaze from the couple. "That is my father and his *wife*." I supposed Mr. Kimble knew about my scandal, then, if he was capable of picking my father from a crowd.

A younger woman stepped out from behind them, her hair the same light strawberry blonde as the older woman's, her gown a regal, white confection that made her look like an angel swathed in golden light.

"And that," Mr. Kimble said, "must be your sister."

"Shall we go?" Elsie gripped my shoulders, her concerned eyes boring into my face. "Why am I even asking? Of course we shall go." She spoke to her husband, her eyes never leaving mine. "Cameron, fetch the carriage please."

Lord Cameron was off at once. What an obedient husband.

"Would you like to sit down?" Elsie asked, her voice growing panicked. "I can fetch a glass of lemonade. Or something stronger?"

I immediately thought of Lady Melbourne throwing punch at a footman. If that had even occurred. Gossip could not be relied upon for accuracy.

"Freya," Elsie said, her voice low and steady, "you are beginning to worry me."

Worry her? Whatever had I done to elicit that response? I had not even said one word...oh. I cleared my throat. "I would like to go home."

I propelled her into action with my words. Her hand came around my arm in a vice-like grip, steering me toward the ballroom exit in a direction that avoided my father and his family. My eyes smarted as I caught knowing glances from the men and women we passed and tears formed in my eyes regardless of how hard I tried to stem them. It was the sudden unexpected presence of my father after four years of not seeing him, and *not* that he brought his real family into my realm, that bothered me so excessively. Nor did it matter that he hadn't written to me in three years.

Not that I was counting, for I did not care.

"I cannot believe the gall of that man," Elsie muttered as we climbed into the carriage. "Selfish, stupid man."

"Elsie," Lord Cameron said gently, his gaze flicking between his wife and me.

I wanted to tell him I was not so fragile, that it felt nice to have someone as angry with my father as I felt, but my mouth remained closed.

We rode home in silence, and I assured both Elsie and Lord Cameron that I would be all right. I simply needed a hot soak and an early night. I felt their pitying gazes warm my back as I mounted the stairs.

It was a relief to be in my own room with the door closed. I leaned back against the hard slab and sank down onto the floor, pulling my knees up and resting my forehead on them. I was too old to sit and cry over my father. I'd had *years* to come to terms with his choices and subsequent abandonment. True, he had once written me letters, years ago, but then he had stopped. If he truly loved me, he wouldn't have given up.

He would not have left.

"Oof!" The door collided with my back. The maid trying to enter uttered a soft curse and tried again. "One moment, please!" I said, pulling myself off the floor and opening the door to let her in.

Mr. Kimble's image floated in my mind as she and another maid began to prepare my bath. If I did not have two women available for the job it would have taken twice as long, and my water would have been twice as cooled. So, there. Take that, Mr. Kimble and your tiresome, thrifty ways.

I sat in the tub after Tilly washed my hair until the water turned cold and I began to shiver, the lavender oil doing very little to calm my nerves. When I finally dressed and climbed into bed, I could not sleep. Images from the ball filtered through my mind over and over again. My father, his wife. Their daughter stepping forward into the glowing candlelight like an ethereal being, absolutely beautiful and quite a few years younger than I. She was a veritable diamond of the first water and was bound to be a smashing hit in London if that was what they were here for.

Oh, heavens. Could that be it? A knot formed in the pit of my stomach and grew at the thought of enduring their presence among my friends and acquaintances for the next few months. If they planned to be here for the entire Season, there was only one answer for it.

I could not be.

CHAPTER 4

I stepped into the breakfast room and silence engulfed me. Elsie sat perched on a chair at the table, her eyebrows pulled together in concern, Lord Cameron's face a mirror image of hers from where he stood at the sideboard.

"Shall I make you a plate?" he asked.

"No, thank you." I picked up a plate and loaded it with my usual fare, ignoring the well-meant attention the Nichols were slathering on me. I sat beside Elsie. Lord Cameron delivered her breakfast and went back to the sideboard to retrieve his own. "Really, I am fine," I said, eyeing Elsie with as much gumption as I could.

"But last night. I cannot even fathom…" She looked to her husband and then back to me. Leaning in, she lowered her voice. "Listen. Cameron has some contacts from his newspaper days. He is willing to make some inquiries to find out what we are dealing with here."

"Actually, that would be really helpful," I said, my shoulders deflating. Elsie clearly had not expected that response, as her honey-colored eyebrows rose a fraction. I lifted my lips in the semblance of a smile. "I want to say it does not matter and I will do what I wish, but what I *really* wish is to not have to see them again. I vow, if I never lay eyes on my father for the rest of my life, I shall die a satisfied woman."

A throat cleared from the doorway, and Elsie and I turned in unison to find my butler, Perkins, standing there, a man behind him.

"I do not know whether to sally forth or tuck tail and run," my father said, belying his words by stepping into the room. Curse Perkins and his absolute disregard for me. He should have waited and announced my father first.

Elsie's hand came under the table and held mine, solidifying her presence and reminding me of the many times she had done so before. If there was one thing I could always count on, it was her unwavering support.

My father's white hair was styled neatly and his clothes looked just as expensive as they had the night before. He'd gained wrinkles around his eyes, but was otherwise unchanged.

"How did you know where to find me?" Not the smartest thing I had ever said, as I recalled the letters he had sent to this address years ago. It had come from my mouth of its own accord, however, and was a suitable replacement for what I truly wished to know: why he had not done so sooner.

"It was not so hard to discover," he said. "I merely asked the right people."

Lord Cameron came to stand behind me in a show of solidarity and support. While I valued his friendship, I did not need his protection. I stood, letting go of Elsie's hand and clasping mine together before me. "What do you need?"

Father's hat spun circles in his hands as he toyed with the brim. My initial reaction was to pity his discomfort but I quickly squashed that feeling away, hardening myself to his plight.

"I hoped to speak to you."

"You are," I said.

"Alone?"

"No," I replied clearly, ignoring his wince. "This is the Nichols' home and I will not ask them to leave. You may speak plainly, sir."

His eyes bore into mine and dread and regret slithered up my spine, much as it did whenever I'd faced my father as a little girl. But he had no control over me now; I was not even his legal daughter. I was *illegitimate*. Fire replaced the discomfort and I gazed back with all of the heat I felt.

He sallied forth. "I hoped we could come to an agreeable arrangement. I've brought Sophie and Adele to Town for the Season and I wished to introduce you."

My heart broke upon hearing their names. I had known of their existence for years, of course, but never before had I known their names. There was something so very real and final about giving someone a name. I could no longer pretend they were unreal—neither could I feign being unaffected.

Silent, warm tears rolled down my cheeks as I severed the last remaining care I had for the man standing on the other side of the breakfast room. "You need to leave," I said with quiet strength.

"But—"

"I am sorry, sir," Lord Cameron said, crossing the room and taking my father's arm. "It's probably best if you go now."

My father yanked his arm free, his eyes searching mine over his shoulder as Lord Cameron escorted him from the room.

"Freya Bee, please," he called.

I squeezed my eyes closed, the pet name from my childhood digging the dagger deeper into my spine. I had to remind myself that he had not used the name in years. Not since I went away to school.

I winced when the front door closed behind my father. Sitting hard on the chair, I was vaguely aware of Elsie's arms coming around me, and I cried into her shoulder, my heart pounding. My father had ruined my life. Surely I owed him nothing. Sitting back in my chair, I wiped my eyes and stared at the congealed butter and toast on my plate.

"What a relief," Lord Cameron said facetiously. "I did not anticipate contacting my old newspaper chums with any excitement. I suppose I need not inquire now that we have learned his intentions."

He was trying to break the tension, I was sure. I stared at him a moment before laughter bubbled up out of my throat. Elsie joined in, and Lord Cameron chuckled.

"I suppose he heard me speak before he entered the room." I wiped my eyes. It was not funny in the least, but Lord Cameron had helped me to relieve some of the tension regardless. "Yet he approached anyway."

Elsie sighed. "He came all this way. I am sure he only wanted to speak his piece."

"And he has. I can walk away now with the comfort of knowing I truly do not need a relationship with him."

Lord Cameron stood from his chair. "I will give you both some time."

Elsie waited until he left before turning toward me. "I know this is perhaps the last thing you would like to hear right now, but I speak from experience when I say holding on to your anger only hurts you, Freya."

I leveled her with a wry look. "Your parents lied about your dowry and tried to force you to wed someone with money, which you *did* end up doing. What your mother did was wrong, but it was nothing like this. She did not try to carry on two families in two separate countries *at the same time*."

"That is true. What you have gone through is horrid, and I could never begin to understand how you have suffered because of it. Yet, I can't help but feel that you would obtain your own sense of resolution if you simply forgave your father. I am not saying you need to have a relationship with him, and you certainly do not need to endure the company of his wife or her daughter, but the forgiveness could help you to let it go."

I stood, her words burning my chest. Hot tears welled in my eyes, and I felt so alone in this trial. I should not have to deal with Father's return by myself, my mother halfway across the country. But I had been alone since the scandal broke, hadn't I?

Suddenly, I knew what I had to do. I was done. With crying, with my father, with the whole of it.

"I am going to Corden Hall," I said. "I will begin packing and shall leave as soon as I can make proper arrangements."

"Whatever are you talking about?" Elsie got to her feet. "You do not need to run away from us, Freya. We can be here for you."

"I am not *running away*," I said acerbically, the accusation hitting a chord within me. "I am going to visit the estate that I own. I have lived off the generosity of others for years, and it is time I support myself. I may not remain there forever, but I should like to see it, and this is as good a time as any. I should like to see the fields of wheat and the red sandstone buildings. My steward has asked me to come and settle some matters, and it seems a prime opportunity to do so. Let *them* have London; I have my own house."

"Very well," she said, her arms falling limp at her sides. "But we only just reunited. Can we accompany you?"

I softened my tone to cushion my words. "You're good to me, Elsie. But I would rather go alone."

Four years of residence in Aunt Georgina's home caused a longer delay in my travels than I had anticipated. I asked Tilly to come with me to Corden Hall and she accepted eagerly. Coco would come also, of course, and it would probably be wise to take a few of the cats off Elsie's hands. There was a stable at

Corden Hall that could possibly house a few felines; the only difficulty was determining which ones to take.

Jasper, the irritable tabby, would be a horrible carriage companion, so he was out. Mabel and Lucille were too old to bother with catching mice and didn't do much beyond sunning in windows or curling up near fireplaces. That left Kitty, Cleo and Max.

I watched Tilly absently as she packed away my gowns and shoes, debating the merits of each cat and which ones I should bring with me. A tap at the door interrupted my musings, and I delivered a strained smile when Elsie stepped inside the room. Things had been different between us since the incident in the breakfast room the week before. I knew she felt like I was running from my problems. She had even said as much. Years before when we first discovered my father's second family and I retreated from Society, she had felt much the same way.

She did not realize at the time that I was not going into hiding, but I was strategizing. I could not face Society until I understood fully what my situation was and how I felt about it. I was simply doing the same thing now. Whether or not she could understand how I felt was irrelevant, for it was how I managed the blows I'd been dealt.

"How is packing coming along?" she asked, coming to sit beside me on the edge of my bed.

"I am trying to decide which cats to take."

"All of them."

I laughed. "Jasper would claw me to death if we were forced to share a carriage ride to Shropshire together."

She moaned. "He is the worst of the lot. Do not tell me you are leaving him here."

"I must! The clawing, remember?"

She pouted. "Very well. I see you have no choice in the matter. How about we make a deal where you take half and leave me half? We can evenly divide Aunt Georgina's babies, for

I know she felt that way about them. Her letters spoke of little else."

Elsie didn't know the half of it. Aunt Georgina simply adored those wretched felines. She *really* loved them as though they were her children. And they loved her back.

Even Jasper.

"I can take three," I agreed. "I know just the ones."

Quiet settled over us as we watched Tilly pack the trunks. "You are really taking everything, aren't you? I wish you didn't have to go."

"I've been here a long time," I reminded her. "I have not had adventures in Spain or India like you. I must have my own now."

She nodded slowly, her eyebrows hitching as she considered my words. "I hadn't thought of it that way before. You haven't really left London much, have you?"

"In the years since our Season I've twice visited my mother in Yorkshire. But nothing more."

"Very well," Elsie said, her energy suddenly lifted. "Which cats are you taking?"

"Kitty, Cleo and Max."

Confused, she glanced around the room. "Is Cleo the gray one?"

"No, that's Mabel. Cleo is black."

Elsie nodded. "And the striped one is?"

"The gray striped one is Kitty. The one with brown and gray stripes is Lucille."

She grinned. "So you are leaving me the lazy cats? How thoughtful of you."

"I figure there should be balance. You get the calm ones to weigh out Jasper."

The door inched open and Coco trotted into the room, coming to rest by my feet. I leaned down and picked up the chocolate-colored terrier, scratching behind her ears. I glanced up at my friend. "I shall miss you, Elsie," I whispered.

Elsie took Coco out of my arms and lovingly scratched her belly. "Then you will simply have to come back and visit."

"Or perhaps you will choose an estate near mine and we can be neighbors permanently."

Elsie stilled, her mouth drooping slightly. "I hadn't thought of that before. Cameron has mainly been looking around the outskirts of London or near his family estate up north."

"Neither of those options sound very agreeable."

"Rosalynn lives up north."

"Oh, pish." I swatted the air, taking my dog back onto my lap. "Rosalynn is constantly coming down to London. I am the one you should settle near."

"I'll speak to Cameron about it," she said. I had a feeling it would not go anywhere, however. Which was fine. I did not want to force anyone to settle in Shropshire. I had never even been there before, myself.

The door flew open and Rosalynn swept inside. My sigh blended with Elsie's and she jumped up to lead Rosalynn to the bed to sit on my other side. Rosalynn pulled her arm free. "I am not an invalid," she said. "Only pregnant."

"What are you doing here?"

"I've brought you a gift." She held out a brown paper-wrapped parcel and I accepted it, one hand holding the gift while the other continued to pet Coco.

"I still cannot believe you are leaving," she continued. "It is wicked of you. I only just arrived and the boys did not get enough of you on Sunday."

"I will visit them again before I go," I said, placing Coco on the floor gently and watching her pad over to her bed near the fire.

"Well, open it!" Rosalyn said with a clap. She grinned, watching me closely.

I untied the string, peeling the paper back to reveal a lumpy pile of dark gray wool.

"Thank you," I said with some uncertainty, lifting the pile of knotted yarn from the paper. A smaller lump fell to the floor and Coco barked at it from across the room. I bent down and swept it up, looking to Rosalynn for some explanation.

She blinked back at me expectantly, and I didn't have the heart to question her. "It's lovely," I said, fingering the thick woolly mass.

"What is it, exactly?" Elsie asked, and I could have kissed her.

Rosalynn laughed. "Isn't it obvious?"

Our blank faces must have answered her question, for she reached forward and lifted the objects from my lap. "Stockings and a scarf. I've been learning to knit."

"That's wonderful," I said, turning the mass in my fingers and trying to find where I was meant to put my foot in the stocking.

"No, that is the scarf. Here are the stockings." She turned them around in her fingers and found the general shape, showing me where I might stuff my foot. "I figured you can imagine my loving embrace as you wrap yourself to keep warm."

"How very sentimental of you, Rosie," I said, trying not to laugh.

Elsie, ever the peacekeeper, reached over me to squeeze Rosalynn's knee. "What a thoughtful gift."

"When do you leave?" Rosalynn asked.

"I've written my steward to warn the household of my arrival and told them to expect me after the first of April. So I suppose I should leave on Monday."

"That is only two days away!" Elsie lamented. "Will you be ready in time?"

Did she mean emotionally? It was unlikely I would ever be ready to leave this home. It was the place where I came into my own sense of self. Aunt Georgina fostered a home full of love and acceptance. It was a place where I could be who I wished without fear of retribution or disapproval. Aunt Georgina took in strays in every meaning of the word and loved them unconditionally, myself included.

The only thing that helped me leave behind this home was that at Corden Hall I would be mistress and could cultivate the same sense of belonging. That, and the fact that Aunt Georgina was no longer here.

"I am ready."

CHAPTER 5

I was *not* ready.

The borrowed traveling carriage wrapped around a simple pleasure garden and rolled to a stop before a high, imposing, red sandstone building with dormer windows at the top and a square, solemn feeling about it. It was not the small, quaint building I had imagined my grandmother inhabiting. To my recollection, I had never met my mother's mother; she died when I was quite young, but I knew she was kind and sweet and this sober house was not at all what I had pictured. The height alone caused me to shrink back against the squabs.

I inched forward again to peek out the window and startled when the door flew open, my coachman's face mirroring my own surprise.

"Sorry, ma'am. Didn't mean to scare you."

Nodding, I accepted his hand to step out of the carriage, my free hand holding up my voluminous skirts. I glanced back at Coco snoozing peacefully on the seat and reached in to pull her out, cradling her in my arms. Tilly stepped out behind me, followed by the cooped-up felines.

The front door of Corden Hall opened and a man stood at

the entryway, likely the butler, his chest puffed out and his nose in the air. I mounted the steps slowly and stepped past him into the house to face a line of servants, the cats circling my feet as I walked. A few maids and footmen stood beside a round woman with a full chatelaine and a tall, gangly woman covered in flour—most likely the cook—held up the end. There were no more than eight servants; Mr. Kimble would approve.

"Welcome, Ma'am," the butler said, turning away from the open door as the coachman carried one of my trunks up the stairs and deposited it on the marble entryway floor with a loud thud.

"I am Harrison." He delivered a low bow. He gestured to the round, white-haired woman with the chatelaine. "This is your housekeeper, Mrs. Lewis. The cook beside her, Mrs. Covey, and the scullery maid, Joan."

I smiled and nodded at each person in turn, hopelessly trying to memorize their names while my fingers absentmindedly stroked Coco's head.

"The housemaids," he continued, "Heather and Hattie. And the footmen, George and Alan. The outside staff is busy at present but can be assembled when you are ready."

I nodded, stepping back. I wanted to say something profound, but my tongue froze, growing thick in my mouth. I was jittery with anticipation. This meeting was a long time in coming, and I hoped beyond measure that seeing my steward in the flesh would not hamper our easy camaraderie. "Aren't we missing someone?"

Harrison exchanged glances with Mrs. Lewis. "Is there another servant you have need of?"

"No, I only meant Mr. Bryce."

Mrs. Lewis stepped forward. "He is gone away on business, ma'am, but he should be back tomorrow. He was sorry to miss your arrival but it was a pressing family matter."

I nodded. I hoped none of his children or—heaven forbid—

grandchildren had taken seriously ill. I must come up with some way to thank him for the work he did in creating such a successful estate out of my inheritance. This house ran like a clock, and it was due to Mr. Bryce's steady guidance.

"I am happy to be here," I said to the gathered group, their round eyes watching me warily. "I appreciate the work you've all done in maintaining my home, and I am sorry it has taken me so long to get here, but until recently I've had a permanent home in London and did not feel a need."

Mrs. Lewis flinched, and I immediately regretted my words. "I only meant I did not have cause to come, for I was—" I clamped my mouth closed. It was not my responsibility to explain myself to the servants, and announcing that I'd been serving as a companion in recent years would not help them to see me in the light of a mistress. I was already struggling to see myself in that capacity as it was.

A scuffle sounded behind me, and I turned. "Oh! This is my maid, Tilly, and these are my cats: Cleo, Kitty, and Max; and my dog, Coco. I hope they might be welcomed here as well."

"Of course, ma'am," Harrison said gallantly. Well, the butler was respectful. Corden Hall had one thing already that Aunt Georgina's house could not claim.

Mrs. Lewis stepped forward. "Allow me to show you to your room." She turned and gestured to the footmen, indicating the trunks left behind by the coachman.

The entry room, though large with intricately carved posts and beams, did not house the staircase. We crossed under an archway and came to a corridor with a large, imposing stairway. The wall had cut out slots that looked down on the foyer and allowed natural light to spill onto the stairs.

Keys dangled on the chatelaine as the housekeeper mounted the stairs, and I followed right behind her. Glancing over her shoulder, Mrs. Lewis said, "The first floor has previously been used as family rooms. The main bedroom has a master and a mistress suite that connect via dressing rooms. We have prepared the mistress suite for you, but if you would like another room you need only say so and the necessary preparations will be arranged."

I nodded, following her down the corridor to a door on the right. The walls and bed coverings were done in a matching rose silk with cream accents and an intricate cream carpet. A dressing table sat near the window with a wardrobe flanking the other side.

"This should do nicely," I said, noting the writing desk against the dark wall and mentally shifting it closer to the window.

"Will the animals reside here with you?" Mrs. Lewis asked with a hint of distaste. She did not seem a fan of me, at present.

At home, the cats had a room of their own. Here, I had thought to put the cats outside if they would be of any use. "Do you already have cats in the stables?"

"Yes, there are sufficient wild animals to take care of the rodents."

So she was not a fan of animals, either, it seemed. That was not likely helping my case. "Then perhaps we will have a room made up for the cats to stay in."

"A room for the cats?" she clarified.

Was that so very odd? There was an entire floor of rooms above me completely empty. "Yes. But Coco will stay with me."

Clearing her throat, she nodded. "I will see what I can do."

The servants left, leaving me with Tilly, the roaming felines, and the sleepy dog. I stepped into the center of the room and turned slowly, taking in every detail before laying Coco at the foot of my bed. This was to be my new home. When would it start feeling like it?

Tilly moved to the wardrobe and began unpacking the trunks while Cleo stretched in the windowsill and Max sniffed around under the bed. Kitty circled my feet, staying close to the side of my leg.

"I feel it too," I said, leaning down to pick her up and stroking her gray-striped fur. "It will be an adjustment for us all."

"I'd say," Tilly said from where she knelt, bent over a trunk of my gowns.

I left Tilly, Coco, and the cats behind to unpack and decided to explore. Beginning with the first floor, I glanced in each room and noted the various style differences, and a few pieces of furniture I wouldn't mind moving to my own bedchamber. By the time I reached the end of the corridor, Harrison found me.

"Dinner is served in the dining room."

I followed him down, not bothering to change for dinner despite his pointed look at my disheveled gown, to say nothing for the state of my hair. But it was my first night in residence, and I simply did not want to bother.

Harrison led me into a room lit with candlelight against the fading sun; a long, solid oak table sat in the center with one place setting at the head. I sat in the chair, diving into a meal full of dishes I was familiar with, but found to be far more flavorful. I was in awe as my mouth erupted with new, remarkable tastes. Could the cook have used magic, perhaps? I had never had such a remarkable culinary experience in my entire life.

My eyes closed as I savored iced ginger cake, rich and airy at the same time.

"Mrs. Covey is superior in the kitchen, is she not?" a deep voice said, catching me off guard.

My eyes flew open to see a tall, handsome gentleman leaning in the doorway, and my bite of cake shot down my throat, sticking unpleasantly. I coughed, hoping to dislodge it in vain. The man crossed the room swiftly, concern clouding his brow as he picked up my water goblet and thrust it into my hand. I gulped down the liquid and sputtered, making a complete fool of myself.

"I apologize, Miss Hurst. I didn't mean to startle you."

"Do not worry, sir," I said, fixing my gaze on the water goblet as one of the footmen—George, I believe—filled it again and I emptied it once more. But how did this man know my name? And why did the butler fail to introduce him?

My composure recovered as much as it could be, I turned to the stranger. What was this man doing in my dining hall? He was dressed plainly, but well, and his gaze fixed on me so steadily it made my heart jump. I glanced behind him but my butler was nowhere to be seen. "How may I help you?"

"Oh, forgive me. I am Mr. Daniel Bryce." He delivered a handsome bow, his medium brown hair flopping over his forehead as he dipped. It was slightly longer than fashionable, but in a rugged way which suited him well. His clothes were well cut, but of practical material. His boots buffed, but not foppish.

And he could not have said *Bryce*.

I guessed his age to be slightly older than my own; he must be the son. I was never informed that my steward's family was in residence. Not that I minded, but it was a strange thing for my steward to leave out of his missives when he had been so thorough in every other regard. I gestured to the chair beside me. "How is your father? I was told he would be returning tomorrow."

He took a seat and George immediately set a plate of food before him. It was as though the servants anticipated that I would invite the man to join me. "I am afraid I do not follow," he said, his eyebrows pulling together. "My father is dead."

"Oh." Well, that is awkward. "Your grandfather, then?"

He gave me an apologetic—if slightly unsure—glance, his eyebrows pulling together. "Dead, too, I'm afraid."

I bit my tongue before *uncle* could spill forth. "Oh, dear.

Perhaps I should cease guessing. Tell me, sir, what is your relation to my steward?"

Mr. Bryce set down his fork and coughed on his bite of ham, pulling a napkin up to his mouth and turning away from me. "I'm sorry to disappoint," he said when he again faced me, his composure restored, "but there are no other Bryces in residence." His hands came up in surrender. "I am your steward."

My mouth fell open, and I raked my gaze over the man beside me. He was tall, handsome, and not nearly old enough to be my father. *This* was the Mr. Bryce I had been corresponding with for the last year? Who sent me such interesting letters, and made me feel listened to? He did not fit the image I had created in my mind of a sweet, elderly gentleman with kind, crinkly eyes and an endearing smile.

My gaze landed on his lips. His smile was wide and unabashed. I would certainly call it endearing. So, perhaps he had *one* of the traits I had been envisioning.

Heat crept up my neck, and I turned my attention to my plate. After my choking fiasco, however, the ginger cake didn't look so appetizing anymore. I pushed it around for a moment with my fork.

What was I doing? I was no simpering miss. I was a grown woman with an estate of my own and this man, regardless of how attractive and decidedly *not* ancient he was, was in my employ. We had a comfortable repertoire over letters, so why should that be any different now? If I could no longer imagine him as a father, perhaps a brother would suffice.

"Have you completed your business?" I asked, rallying my nerves. "I was told you had urgent family matters to attend to."

His gaze, previously fixed on me, flitted away before coming back and resting on my hands, clasped on the edge of the table. "Things are well in hand," he answered ambiguously.

"Very good. And do you..." I cleared my throat. "Do you reside *in* this house?"

Silence sat in the room. A smile played at Mr. Bryce's lips and I immediately glanced away from them, moving to gaze at his eyes instead. "Yes. I have a room on the second floor. It is above the family rooms."

Nodding, I considered the propriety of the matter. He was, it seemed, reading my mind.

"I had not before considered the matter of a chaperone," he said delicately. "Perhaps I ought to move to the stables."

"You cannot sleep with the animals," I said, disgusted.

"No," he chuckled, a low throaty sound that flipped my stomach. "I would not find a horse to be a pleasant roommate. But the people of Linshire are not as progressive, perhaps, as those in London. And there is a handsome set of rooms above the stables which are not in use. I would be quite comfortable there."

And my reputation would remain intact. I did not voice the conclusion, but we were of the same mind. There was enough fodder in my history to feed the gossip mill of Linshire if it were to be discovered. There wasn't much sense in adding to it before I had the chance to make a decent name for myself here. I wanted, badly, to argue that as a spinster firmly on the shelf, it mattered not what the people of Linshire thought of me. But I refrained. He knew my feelings on the matter. I had not held much back in our correspondence.

But then again, I had thought I was discussing my life with a fatherly sort of man. Not *this*.

I looked up again as Mr. Bryce finished his dinner and shot me a smile. A handsome, rugged smile that filled me with warmth, taking me by surprise. Immediately I got to my feet, nearly knocking the chair back.

This was all very foreign to me. My heart beat rapidly as I sought something to say.

"Thank you, I shall—oof!" I backed into a decorative table, wincing as my side scraped the corner. The footman leapt over and stopped the decanter from spilling dark red wine all over the blue carpet as Mr. Bryce jumped from his chair, his hands out as though he meant to steady me. I sidestepped him, avoiding the contact I was sure would not do me any good, and made it to the doorway. "I hope you sleep well. I shall see you tomorrow."

I bobbed a quick curtsy and turned away, running to the stairs and away from the horrid, embarrassing scene I had created in the dining room. Well, if nothing else, I was sure to have made an impression on my butler, footman and steward, an impression which was sure to make its rounds among the servants by morning.

Groaning, I slipped inside my room and closed the door, blowing a piece of hair from my face. I glanced down at my dirt-caked traveling gown and old boots.

An impression, indeed. Only, not the impression I hoped to give. All three cats approached me and rubbed against my legs, enfolding me in comfort. I could hear Aunt Georgina's voice clearly in my mind, *You be you, darling. For there is no other you in the entire world.*

Well, Corden Hall was going to receive *me*, in all of my glory, whether they wanted to or not. Me, my cats, and my dog.

Where on earth *was* my dog?

CHAPTER 6

Sunlight filtered through the bed hangings and hit me square in the eye. I squinted, rolling away from the harsh light and into the cool darkness on the other side of my bed. My face landed directly in a pile of black fur.

Cleo hissed before leaping from the bed. I sat up quickly, noting where the other two felines rested so as not to repeat the experience. My chest heaving, I leaned back against the headboard, considering Max curled up by my feet and Kitty not far from him. I had a feeling the cats had staked their claim on my bed and it would likely be pointless to try and move them to a separate room.

Quite the opposite of Coco, who had claimed a different bedchamber all to herself.

I climbed out of bed and pulled on the bell to send for Tilly.

Crossing to the door which adjoined the mistress and master rooms, I peeked through the dressing room and found Coco curled into the center of the massive four poster bed, snoring happily. She had slipped into the master's room the day before, and both of the times I'd tried to bring her back into my bed chamber, she lasted mere minutes before leaving for her own again.

It hardly mattered. As long as I was in residence, then the master's suite was destined to remain empty. I'd had my chance at marriage during my Season and I had soundly turned it down. Coco may as well take advantage of the large, plush, empty feather mattress.

By the time my maid arrived, I had investigated the writing desk and dressing table, and thoroughly brushed through my bright red hair.

"Did you sleep well?" I asked as she pulled a dress from the wardrobe and began to help me out of my night clothes.

"Yes, miss. The rooms are warm here."

I glanced at her over my shoulder. "Were the servants' rooms cold in London?"

She avoided my eyes so I turned to face her head on. "Tilly, why did you never mention this before?"

"They weren't *cold* exactly, simply not as warm as they are here." Her mouth clamped shut, and no matter how hard I stared at her, she was not going to betray more information. I needed to write to Elsie about the matter immediately. I knew Perkins did not like me much, but I no longer had to live under the same roof as him. If he was skimping on fires for the servants, I was going to make sure something was done.

"How are the other servants receiving you?" I asked instead.

"I've no complaints," she said simply. "They asked me all sorts of questions about London. Most of them have never left Linshire in their whole lives."

"What a small existence."

She nodded. "And it makes them ever so curious."

"I'd imagine so," I said, watching in the mirror as Tilly took my wavy hair and wrapped it into a knot behind my head. My hair had never been particularly obedient, but Tilly had a way of fastening it that at least kept most of it intact. There would always be stray strands that got away, but I was never one for an uptight, polished appearance. Not that I had much say in the matter with the unruly hair I'd inherited.

Shiny strawberry blonde hair in a perfectly styled coiffure came, unbidden, to my mind. I stared into the mirror imagining how different I should look if I was born with strawberry blonde hair. It was hard to tell if the heavy feeling deep in my gut was rooted in envy or discomfort, but either way I did not like it.

Sophie and Adele. It plagued me that I did not know which name belonged to my father's wife and which to his daughter. It plagued me even greater that the matter bothered me at all.

"Miss?" Tilly pulled me from my melancholy thought. She stood behind me with her hands clasped, my hair finished and my toilette complete. "Should I bring you a breakfast tray or would you like to go down to the breakfast room? Mrs. Covey prepares a breakfast every morning for Mr. Bryce and the servants."

Mr. Bryce, another person I'd rather not think about. But if I took a tray in my room, would he think I was trying to avoid him? He would be correct, of course, but I could not give that impression on my very first morning at Corden Hall.

I was the mistress, after all.

And anyway, he may not plan to eat in the dining room with me.

"I'll go down for breakfast," I said bravely.

I was not so brave as I descended the stairs, however. I followed Tilly's directions to locate the breakfast room, and then hovered outside the door considering how I should greet my steward. He was not a member of the family, but neither was he a servant. Did I say, "Good morning, sir?" Or would it be better to go with a more relaxed approach of, "Good morning, Mr. Bryce?"

"Good morning, Miss Hurst."

I jumped at the close proximity of Mr. Bryce's voice and

spun, coming face to cravat with the man at once. "Oh! Yes. 'Tis morning."

I lifted my face to see his smiling eyes, much too close to allow normal breathing. Yes, I should have gone with the relaxed approach. He was bound to think me silly.

"Are you planning to go in?" he asked.

"Yes. Are you?" I sounded like a complete ninny. What on earth had gotten into me?

His gaze flicked to the door and back to me. "I would not wish to intrude, Miss Hurst. I can eat downstairs."

The man was a gentleman. He had surely been used to eating in dining rooms for the duration of his life, and clearly did so at Corden Hall before I arrived. There was no reason he should cease doing so now. Besides, with his company mealtimes were bound to be less lonesome.

My heart raced and I turned, opening the door and doing my best to sound nonchalant. "There is no reason why you cannot eat in here." I moved to the sideboard and Mr. Bryce followed. He tried to take my plate, but I put him off. "I have been getting my own breakfast for years, and I am not about to stop now. Thank you for offering, though."

He looked down at me as though I had grown an extra head. Had I not made my views clear in our letters? Surely he'd met an independent woman before. I loaded a piece of toast and coddled egg onto my plate, skipping the meat options. Mr. Bryce filled his own with kippers and I tried not to look disgusted.

"You don't like fish?" he asked, apparently reading my mind again.

"Not my favorite." I took a seat at the round table, pouring myself a cup of tea and preparing it with sugar but no cream.

"Mrs. Covey makes the most delightful blueberry muffins, but sadly there are none today. Take my word for it," he said, sitting beside me at the table, "you'll never have a muffin more moist."

"I believe you." I tucked into my meal, sipping tea between bites of toast. "Now, do you have anything to report? Your last letter indicated some discord between a few of the tenant families?"

He turned to face me, a soft smile on his lips—lips that I was decidedly avoiding looking at. His eyes, I could see now in the morning light, were pale green rimmed in darker green. They were handsome, to say the least, so I focused on my egg as he spoke. "I have a general rule not to discuss business over meals."

That was not what I expected. I glanced up sharply. "Ever? You are in earnest?"

"Yes. I am sorry. I don't *ever* discuss business over meals. But I would be happy to meet with you later this morning to go over a few things."

"Very well." It was not as though I had anything else to occupy my time. I wanted a thorough evaluation of the books, of course. And at some point, I should have a full tour of the house. But neither of those things were very pressing.

"Have you been to Linshire before?" Mr. Bryce asked.

So he could speak over breakfast, only not about estate business? Interesting. "No," I answered. We had driven through the small town on our way to the estate but we did not stop to look around. "I have never been to any part of Shropshire. I grew up in Kent and have lived in London for the past four years. The most I've traveled has been the occasional trip to Yorkshire to see my mama."

He nodded. "I have a good friend in Yorkshire. Beautiful country up there."

"Beautiful country here as well," I countered. "The scenery on my trip here was unrivaled."

"This side of the country is breathtaking. Though I feel I must admit I am slightly biased."

"It is not so terrible to be loyal."

His face turned stony and I could feel the air shift as he stiffened. "My loyalty is not in question here."

My skin prickled, his demeanor icy, and I regretted my words. If only I knew what I had said to offend him so.

We finished our meal in relative silence, Mr. Bryce standing before his plate was cleared, and offering me a warm smile, his good nature restored. The way he looked at me penetrated my defenses and left me breathless, and I did not know how to feel about that. No man had elicited such a response from me before, *ever*.

"I will meet you in the study at ten?" he asked.

I nodded as he swept from the room. The clock on the mantle indicated that I had nearly an hour before our appointment, and the windows flanking the fireplace beckoned me with warm sunlight. "Alan," I said, hoping I had the correct name for this footman. "I would like to look at the gardens. Would you direct me?"

"Yes'm."

I followed him out into the front drive. It was chilly in the spring morning. It would have been prudent to wear a shawl. I was never overly concerned with freckles, so I did not bother with bonnets in general, but warmth was a different matter altogether.

"The gardens to the front of the house are simple," Alan said, sweeping an arm over the front drive. "The pleasure gardens in the rear of the house have a lot of flowers. Ladies seem to like the ones in the back more."

"Thank you, Alan. How very astute you are."

His cheeks blushed to match his red hair. I sincerely hoped my own cheeks did not turn such an obnoxiously bright shade when I blushed, but as I had never been around a mirror at the precise moment I'd been embarrassed, I truly did not know. Alan, however, seemed to turn all one color, which blended from his cheeks up to his hair. I dismissed him to ease both of our comfort levels and made my way around to the back of the house. A large, well-kept stable yard was off to my right with a large paddock to its side. Horses whinnied as men bustled about, and I turned toward the garden, beautifully displayed just behind me.

The grounds were open, vibrant, and reached my soul, filling me with a warmth that could not be owed to the sun alone. The pleasure garden was well-manicured and covered in flowers of multiple variations, the bright colors popping. My mother would simply adore such a garden.

Short hedges outlined the garden, and I let myself in through a waist-level wrought iron gate, clicking it shut behind me. A gravel path forked in two different directions and I turned right, following the shrubbery around the perimeter of the manicured space. The majority of the flowers looked nearly ready to bloom, but not quite there yet. I cut through the center of the garden and came to a fountain that acted as a focal point, surrounded by rows of greenery and rose bushes. The object in the fountain looked to be a woman and a man dancing together. It was romantic, and sweet. I felt a strong desire to have it ripped from the ground and replaced with something a little less romantic. Like animals, perhaps. Or maybe just a water feature without a figurine at all.

I needed to find out if the piece had any significance or if it would be acceptable to remove.

"Miss Hurst!" a voice called from the house. I turned to find Tilly rushing toward me, my shawl draped over her arm.

I met her at the gate. "Thank you, Tilly," I said, reaching for the shawl and tossing it around my shoulders. "I was wishing for this mere moments ago. How did you know?"

She shrugged. "I was told to fetch it to you. It's chilly out here, miss. I best be getting back inside."

She bustled back toward the house, and I pulled the forest green shawl tighter around my shoulders. Returning my attention to the flowers, I took the path to the left. It was not a symmetrical garden in the truest form. While the fountain remained a main focal point and everything seemed balanced from there out, the right path had led me in a circle around the perimeter, but the left side did not. It reached halfway around the flowers, but then the path veered away from the garden, running perpendicular to the house. The hedges continued to act as a barrier, growing steadily higher until all views were obstructed outside of the narrow lane and it stopped dead at a wooden door, a large iron handle dangling free with no visible lock.

I pulled on the handle, but it did not budge. The heavy wooden slab had not been moved in some time, it appeared. I tugged harder, using every bit of strength I possessed until I managed to move it slightly. I dragged the heavy door open enough to slip inside and immediately caught my breath.

A small, circular garden with an abundance of greenery and wildflowers spread before me with a simple stone bench in the center. It was a veritable oasis, and I was struck by the beauty and simplicity of its design. The hedge wall was taller than I, wild and untamed. It was thick enough to block the light and view outside of the circle. I stepped into the center, lowering myself onto the stone bench with quiet reverence. Whoever created this space had an absolute affinity for solitude and peace, of that I was absolutely certain.

Quiet calm settled over me, and I pulled my shawl tighter to ward off the chill. The house was stunning, to say nothing of the surrounding grounds. Though no master or mistress had been in residence for the last twenty years, the servants had not allowed the house to fall into disrepair as was so frequently the case in similar situations. Though *why* mother never wanted to come reside here was a mystery. Her own mother had left me the estate at her death, so it stood to reason that Mama would be familiar with the house. But the one time I mentioned it as an optional home, she had shot down the suggestion immediately. I did not press her further, for at the time, her plan to stay with Aunt Marianne and leave me in London had suited me just fine.

Now, I was going to press.

I stood up, glancing once more around the hidden oasis before slipping back through the door and down the gravel walkway. I paused in view of the ivory statue. My first order of business would be that; I must find a way to replace it.

I could not help but appreciate my situation here. The journey to Corden Hall and recent occupancy had culminated into something of an unrealistic fairy tale. If one did not count my odd behavior at dinner the night previous or at breakfast this morning with Mr. Bryce, then it was clear that things were going well and Corden Hall was a lovely place to be.

I found a door to the side of the house and let myself into the kitchen, effectively halting all work the moment I was noticed. "Do not mind me," I said sheepishly, glancing around fervently for the stairs. "I will find my way around sooner or later."

"Allow me," a housemaid said, stepping forward.

I could not remember her name for the life of me, so I simply nodded.

She led me through the servants' dining room to a staircase at the far side of the room and up onto the ground floor. "Thank you," I said, "That will be all."

She curtseyed and went away, her black curls bobbing along with her steps.

"Were you lost?" a deep voice asked from the other end of the corridor. I pivoted to find Mr. Bryce standing in a doorway, his hand resting lightly on the handle. "Perhaps we should schedule a tour of the house before we tackle the rest of the estate business."

"Is it past ten? I got caught up walking the grounds, and I fear I did not watch the time."

He glanced over his shoulder before pulling the door shut and stepping into the corridor. "It is half past now, but it is no matter." He crossed the length of the corridor. He genuinely seemed unperturbed, and I found myself relieved, grateful for his easy demeanor. "Do you ride?"

"Yes, but not particularly well."

He came to stand beside me. "It is a fine day. Shall we begin our tour with an extensive overview of the grounds?"

"I'm not sure that my riding abilities encompass an *extensive* tour, but I am willing to try."

"Very good." He grinned. I stared at his uneven, white teeth held in a crooked smile. "I will meet you down here in half an hour?"

I nodded, keenly aware that he'd caught me staring at his mouth. Why was I so drawn to this man? He was handsome, sure, but not more striking than any other man of my acquaintance. His manners, while kind and familiar, were not overtly flirtatious either, yet he had a knack for putting me to the blush.

It was an unfamiliar feeling, and I did not like it one bit.

Tilly pulled my old riding habit from the wardrobe and helped me into it. I had not had much use of it since Aunt Georgina's death, and it fit a little snug. But, for a simple ride in the countryside, it would do.

Coco trotted toward my feet, and I bent to scratch her head. "You would not be able to keep up with us today, I think. But perhaps I can take you out to the garden later."

She tilted her head before turning back for her bedchamber. The poor thing had been melancholy since Aunt Georgina's demise. While she was growing older, she was not ancient yet and there was still life within her. I would find something to excite her once again; I was determined.

CHAPTER 7

"Are all of these horses mine?" I asked with no little amazement. The stables were full to the brim, neighing and muffled hoofbeats intertwining in an equine symphony. While I was no great judge of prime horseflesh, I could appreciate a clean set of lines like any well-bred adult. I turned in a slow circle. The air held a sense of industry as stable workers moved this way and that, methodically working down the line of stalls with clear purpose. "And is it always this busy?"

Mr. Bryce chuckled, a dimple appearing on his cheek that struck me at once. Apprehension planted a small seed within me. It had been years since my heart had raced at a man's smile, the disloyal organ.

I turned my head away, pretending to admire the dappled gray that was saddled for me. I ran my fingers through her white mane and looked in her dark eyes.

"There are a few horses the main house utilizes for work, but the majority are mine," Mr. Bryce said as I stared at the coarse, straw-like hair on the horse's neck. I bravely turned back to face him and he regarded me closely. "I did mention it when I first began here. I deduct boarding and all of their food from my pay."

I tried to chuckle nonchalantly but it came out more like a trill. Clearing my throat, I ignored my warming cheeks. "I recall the conversation. I suppose I did not realize how many horses you brought with you when you came to run Corden Hall."

"I only brought two horses originally. The rest have been acquired during my time here."

"To what purpose?" I asked, stepping away from the horse as a stable hand placed the mounting block beside her.

He grinned, the sneaky dimple making an appearance once more. "I dabble in horse breeding, I suppose."

"How does one *dabble* in such a thing?" I pulled myself up onto the steady horse and led her out of the stable, Mr. Bryce following on his own steed not far behind.

He reined in beside me. "That is my humble way of saying I am an aspiring horse breeder. I've had some victories, and many more failings. But, one way or another, I will find success in this endeavor." He smiled modestly. "Eventually."

"It is good to set a goal," I agreed. "You should have something to work toward. If this is what you want to do with your life, then it is admirable. And by the looks of it, you've got your stock off to a great start."

"Do you know much about horses?"

"Not even a little," I said unrepentantly, eliciting a chuckle from my steward. "Now, where shall we begin?"

He straightened in the saddle, a businesslike demeanor settling onto his shoulders. "I thought we should ride around the perimeter so I can show you the extent of your lands. We'll pass by each tenant farm. I can name them off to you now, but it may take some time before you remember everything."

"So a basic overview?"

"Yes, precisely."

Tucking an errant lock of hair behind my ear, I swept my arm before me. "Lead the way, sir."

We spent the better part of an hour trotting through field after field. Mr. Bryce pointed out the different grains we grew and the men who were in charge of them. A few of the farmers regarded me warily as I smiled down at them from atop my horse.

"They aren't the friendliest lot," I said once we moved out of earshot.

Mr. Bryce opened his mouth, glanced at me, and closed it once more.

"What is it?" I asked.

He shrugged, pulling his horse away from the wheat field and toward a thick wooded area.

"Mr. Bryce, is there something you would like to say?"

"No, ma'am. I would not like to say anything at all."

I rephrased. "Please?"

It had the desired effect. He pulled his horse to a stop, breathing out a longsuffering sigh. "You are going to force me to speak, aren't you?"

"I cannot *force* you, sir."

His raised eyebrow contradicted me. I recalled my role as his employer, a fact I had not considered until this moment.

Regretfully, I tilted my head. There was an easy camaraderie between us, and I did not want my authority to place a wedge there. "Perhaps I should let it go."

"Perhaps," he agreed, his eyes seeming to scrutinize me. "But I have the distinct feeling you are not one to let things go easily."

My cheeks flushed. Was I as red in the face as Alan, the footman, had been that morning? I tried not to think about that, for it only warmed my cheeks further. I trained my gaze on my mare's stringy mane and nudged her forward. "I can when I wish to."

"I have always been honest with you, Miss Hurst. I will not cease now." His tone was steady. "The tenants are not unfriendly; they are rather intimidated."

I glanced at him. It was clear he was in earnest.

"It is the truth," he continued. "Did you not notice Tomlinson?"

"The man with the brown cap?" I clarified. "He was very polite."

"Precisely."

"I do not understand you."

He chuckled. "That man swears worse than a sailor. He reined in his tongue and showed a deference which shocked me. I am convinced the men don't know what to do with a woman in charge. Especially a woman with opinions."

"His cottage roof."

"Yes," Mr. Bryce nodded. "His cottage roof."

I felt my neck warm. I had commanded the man to repair his roof. With weather as changeable as ours, it was folly to leave a roof so badly patched. I was positive the interior of the cottage was lined with buckets and bowls to catch drips. Mr. Tomlinson had been agreeable about the changes. That could have been due to my insistence on paying for the repair. Though, I imagined Mr. Bryce would have made the same offer.

"It is not very often these men are told what to do by a beautiful woman of high rank. It is unsettling for them, but they will adjust in time."

I turned away, my pulse racing. Stomping down the compliment, I refused to let it go to my head. Beauty was irrelevant when one considered my parentage. I was no better than any of these men, only richer.

"It is about time we are heading back," I said. "Let us return."

Mr. Bryce turned his horse to keep pace with mine as we

trotted along the perimeter of the woods. "That might be difficult."

"Why?"

"Because," he said, slowing my horse as he stalled his own and setting his unnerving, amused smile on me. "We are going the wrong way."

"You've a visitor, Mr. Bryce," Harrison said the moment we walked through the front door.

"I'll see him in the study."

Harrison cleared his throat and Mr. Bryce turned accordingly, raising his eyebrows in inquiry. As the steward, Mr. Bryce was the highest-ranking paid member of the household, and it did not appear as if Mr. Bryce had any trouble acting his rank.

Harrison said, "She is waiting in the drawing room with her maid."

Mr. Bryce stilled. His throat worked, and it felt as though he purposely kept his glance from hitting me as he nodded once distinctly and swept toward the drawing room.

I watched him go and tried not to care that he had not invited me to join him. While it was my home, he had been given free rein of it for a year. The habit to receive a caller in the drawing room must have been well ingrained, odd as it was. I tried not to feel disappointed. I would have liked to meet a member of the local society.

Unless this mystery visitor was *not* a member of local society.

I turned to Harrison. "Will you have Tilly sent up?"

I took the stairs with haste. If Tilly was able to help me change quickly enough then perhaps I could seat myself in a place to meet Mr. Bryce's visitor on her way out. It was childish perhaps, but I merely wished to assuage my curiosity, nothing more.

Tilly had a gown prepared and helped me clear the riding dust as I changed from my habit. She brushed and repinned my hair in silence, and I found myself brooding slightly, for no apparent reason.

What did it matter if Mr. Bryce chose to see another woman and not inform me of who she was? His quick departure indicated he had some clue as to who may have called, and no one had explicitly said it was a social call.

Either way, it was none of my business. I had known Mr. Bryce for one day.

No, that was inaccurate. I had known him for an entire year, and our letters led me to feel that I knew the man well, but that did not mean he owed me anything beyond what I paid him for.

By the time I finished dressing, I was decided. It was none of my concern who Mr. Bryce met with unless he chose to inform me. I paid him to manage my estate so I wouldn't need to. I did not intend to stand in his way.

Taking the stairs up to the next floor, I purposely put more distance between myself and the front door. The carpet that ran the length of the corridor was worn, nearly threadbare in parts. I followed it to the end of the corridor, exploring each bedchamber one at a time, with Coco on my heels. My grandparents had interesting taste in design, if they were to blame for the hideous colors and heavy furniture adorning each of the rooms. But some of the curtains had to be blamed on more distant relatives, for they were nearly falling apart. There was a chair in one bedchamber leaning upon three legs and a bed in another without any mattress.

There seemed to be bits and pieces of broken or faulty furniture or decor in each and every room, but I imagined it had not mattered much with the lack of inhabitants over the past two decades. It took a moment for me to understand what was missing from the corridor, but deeper concentration revealed the lack of portraits or framed landscapes one would usually find breaking up the space between doors.

Halfway down the corridor, I froze in the doorway of the next chamber. It opened toward the top of the stairs and I felt vulnerable, for anyone could mount those stairs and find me idling in the doorway at any moment. My hand rested on the door handle and I recognized the need to close it right away but found myself pasted to the spot instead. 'Twas the only room on this floor without a noticeable fault. The bed was neatly made and the surfaces free from clutter, the only exception being the writing desk. It was placed before the window and littered with papers. A few books stacked on the corner looked near to toppling over.

Coco let herself into the room and began sniffing near the wardrobe. I wanted to pull her out but could not bring myself to step further into the room.

"Coco," I hissed. "Come, girl." I could not whistle without alerting the household of my location.

A framed portrait on the table beside the bed caught my eye. It was turned away just enough that I could make out nothing more than the outline of a woman. I stepped forward to take a closer look when a voice from the corridor startled me.

"I have moved into the rooms above the stables, but have not yet gathered all of my things. I will remove my belongings by the end of the day."

I spun to see Mr. Bryce, his green eyes lit with irritation. A smile touched his lips briefly but did not remain.

I stepped back, further into the room. No other course of action was available to me as the door was blocked by the man, and his proximity was unsettling. "I apologize, Mr. Bryce. You may take your time in the endeavor. I am not in any hurry to see the room evacuated."

"Are you not?"

Swallowing, I shook my head slowly. I was unused to the brisk manner in which he spoke. Was his irritation due to the guest he'd just entertained, or to finding me in his bedchamber? Likely the latter. "I have been exploring this part of the house. I did not consider that I would be intruding on your personal space."

His expression showed subtle disbelief, but I stood firm. Mr. Bryce might be a gentleman fallen in station, but he was still an employee. I had every right to be in his room. Regardless of its accidental nature.

For all of my mighty thoughts, I was not eager to remain where I was. I whistled sharply and Coco ran to my feet. "If you would excuse me," I said, stepping forward, hoping the action would push him from the doorway.

He was slow to respond, causing me to brush his shoulder on my way past. It left a burning sensation in my arm and I rubbed it to dissipate the feeling before I bent down to pick up my dog.

Mr. Bryce spoke, forcing me to halt just above the stairs. "May we postpone our meeting? I have some matters of business that cannot wait."

My foot hovered over the step as my free hand gripped the railing. I looked over my shoulder. "Yes, tomorrow should be fine." I turned and descended the stairs without another word, but the look Mr. Bryce had directed my way burned into my mind and refused to depart. Whether anger or frustration played a part, I didn't know, but his restraint was evident. I could not quite name the expression, and that fact haunted me more than anything else.

I met Harrison on the main level and asked, "How far away is Linshire?"

"A fifteen-minute ride by carriage."

"And the closest estate?"

Harrison rocked back on his heels, looking to the ceiling for the answer. "That would depend on which way you traveled. The Gromley farm is northward, and south runs you to Fairlinn Court."

I searched my brain for the name Gromley, but came up short. I had not met any Gromleys on my tour that morning. "The Gromley farm is not one of ours, correct?"

He nodded. "Correct. Mr. Gromley is a gentleman farmer but deals mostly in sheep."

"Thank you, Harrison." I dismissed the butler and headed toward my chamber. I was beginning to feel overwhelmed by the large house and how little I knew about the area. I was ready to spend the remainder of the day with a good book, Coco, and my cats.

CHAPTER 8

I was unprepared at dinner to face the jovial Mr. Bryce, as he had bordered on surly during our encounter earlier in the day. Indeed, I had wondered if he would even dine with me after the episode in his bedchamber, or if he would instead choose to remove downstairs to eat with the servants. But upon finding him awaiting me to go into dinner, my chest warmed and my spirits lifted. Speaking to Mr. Bryce was far preferable to keeping my own company.

He helped me to the head of the table, taking the chair just to my right, an amiable smile on his lips.

"Did you have a productive day?" I inquired just as he lifted a soup spoon to his lips.

He nodded, wiping his mouth. "I took the liberty of preparing a few charts to show you the changes we've made at Corden Hall since my arrival. If you have the time tomorrow, I would love to go over it with you."

"I've nothing else to do."

He looked at me sharply as though he knew something I did not. It was not the first time I had felt that Mr. Bryce was hesitant to voice his opinion. It was rather trying, to be honest.

"Can we not speak plainly with one another?" I begged. "We've been doing just that in our correspondence, and I feel it would be significantly simpler if I was not trying to constantly guess what you are thinking."

He replied softly, "I understand the frustration."

My eyebrow lifted of its own accord. I did nothing to bring it back down.

"Very well," he said, lifting his hands in surrender. "I only wonder if you might be busy tomorrow with calls."

"What calls? I know no one in Linshire."

"Correct. But word has spread around Linshire that the owner of Corden Hall—a single woman, even—is in residence. If I know the people here, they will be sending around the welcoming committee quickly."

I could not tell if I felt more irritation or anxiety at the prospect of a welcoming committee.

"You do not seem pleased," Mr. Bryce said, setting down his spoon.

"I am not fond of strangers. Or unannounced visits."

He peered at me thoughtfully. "I had planned to go into Stoneford in the afternoon on business, but I could postpone another day."

What was he suggesting? I might not *enjoy* social visits, but I did not need anyone to hold my hand. I had been independent for the better part of four years and I was not about to shrink with fear. "I shall be fine. What is the nature of your business?"

That did not seem to be the question he expected. "There is a man in Stoneford selling a mare I've had my eye on. I need to negotiate a fair price."

"Then you must go."

He studied me, and I found myself squirming in my chair. I cleared my throat. "And this mare is important to your work?"

"She could be," he said. "I believe with her blood I can produce top rate foals."

"As opposed to the other mares you have in the stables?"

He smiled. "It would be difficult to explain. But yes, she is superior."

I shook my head. "I know so little about business."

"And I"—he grinned—"cannot discuss it further. I believe you remember my rule."

I sipped a spoonful of soup. "Yes, I remember. No discussing business over food."

One concise nod and Mr. Bryce delved into his meal once more. I could not blame the man. His life revolved around running my estate and surrounding land, not to mention his free time taken up with horse breeding. It was fair that he expected one time of day where he could just *be*.

"Now," he said. "Tell me about your family. Your mother resides in Yorkshire, you said?"

I froze. I had mentioned her in a letter many months back. Could Mr. Bryce know of the scandal with my father? He was a gentleman, and would therefore have relationships and connections within Society.

I ventured forth cautiously. "She lives with her sister, yes."

"And are you able to see her often?"

"I've seen her twice in the last four years. It is more, I gather, than many are able to accomplish, so I take my holiday visits with satisfaction."

"Yes," he said. "That is a positive attitude to affect."

"She was not interested in coming to Corden Hall when I inquired last, but I have dispatched another letter renewing the invitation." I tried to turn the conversation. "Do you have family nearby?"

"No."

"So you understand. Are you able to get away and visit them?"

Mr. Bryce turned away, a tight smile on his lips. "There is no one to visit, so I need not concern myself with family."

That was a bleak perspective. Or one hardened through time alone. Pity snaked into my thoughts before I shoved it out again. I despised when others pitied me. I guessed Mr. Bryce and I had a connection, in that sense.

"On my exploration earlier, I did discover something of interest."

He turned interested eyes on me and a smile revealed his dimple. I trained my blushing face toward my plate. It was not my finest moment to be caught snooping in his bedchamber, but it could not be undone. No use pretending it hadn't happened.

"What is it you found?"

"Quite a lot of disarray," I said.

"I cannot speak for the man who held this position before me, but I did not see the need to spend money replacing carpets and furniture when there was no family in residence and none expected for the foreseeable future. But, to be quite honest, I have not felt comfortable leaving such a lovely home in this condition any longer." He caught and held my gaze. "It was one of the reasons I recommended your visit, if you recall."

I did not recall that particular reason, but he could have slipped it in amongst the other business items we'd discussed.

"But I feel inclined to remind you that we are veering dangerously close to discussing business."

I tried to swallow my amusement. This man was certainly interesting. His rule to avoid mixing business with his meals was strange, but I would do my best to respect it.

Having both spent some time in London, we discussed our favorite sights and museums. He waxed long on the superior qualities of country living, and I agreed that a slower pace had much to be desired.

We withdrew to the drawing room following dinner and Mr. Bryce asked if I played any musical instruments.

"I can play the pianoforte reasonably well."

"Would you care to play for me?"

I found the pianoforte in good condition. The music selection was a tad outdated, but it would do well enough. I played for the better part of an hour, losing myself a few times in the music. I was no master by any means—I did not come close to Rosalynn's skill in music—but I was competent for an evening of simple entertainment.

"That was lovely," Mr. Bryce said when I stepped away from the instrument. I delivered a playful curtsy and took my seat across from him on a plush violet armchair.

"Thank you, Mr. Bryce."

I smiled at him, comfortable and secure. His green eyes were trained on me and though a few yards of space and a luxurious carpet separated us, I felt a connection with this man. He was— dare I hope—the brother figure I had never had. He was kind and reliable. Through our correspondence, we had developed a level of trust and companionship I had grown to appreciate.

I only hoped he felt the same way. The sporadic feelings of attraction and increased heart rate were behind me. I could not control my natural reactions, but I could steer them in the proper course. Mr. Bryce was like a brother. And as such he would stay.

"I have been thinking," he said, pulling me from my musings. "Perhaps you would be comfortable calling me Daniel? I am afraid to admit that I do not think of you as Miss Hurst."

Did my face show the surprise I felt? This was a bold request, to say the least. "I would like that. I only wonder if it would send the wrong message."

"To whom?"

"Neighbors, the staff."

He seemed to consider my words. "I do agree it could convey the wrong message. Perhaps we could be more formal when in company."

If we only used given names in private, then there was little harm in it. I had to agree with the man; we'd built such a connection through our letters that we felt close to family already. It was unorthodox, perhaps, but so was every other aspect of my life at present. I had dined with my steward, for heaven's sake. "We shall be working together quite closely. Perhaps that would be a convenient course of action."

Daniel's answering grin was warm. I tried to laugh off the discomfort it caused within me. "For now, however, I shall retire for the evening."

We stood in unison and he bowed. "Goodnight, Freya."

I reached the door, glancing over my shoulder. "Goodnight, Daniel."

Daniel had been correct in his assumption that the women of Linshire would soon flock to me. I had caller after caller all morning, and at the rate they were arriving, I was going to be stuck in the drawing room for the remainder of the day.

I had to skip our morning meeting due to the arrival of the vicar's wife and her three children. They were followed by Mrs. Hathaway and her daughters, Laura and Jane, whom I felt I would never, ever find any sort of connection with. They were young, sixteen and seventeen if I had to guess, and the frilliest, most uninspiring creatures I had met in quite some time. They inundated me with questions about London and it was all I could do to try and slip a word in during their rapid inquisition. Mrs. Hathaway seemed content to sit back and watch her insipid children with a self-contented smile on her round face.

I would never understand the pride of some mothers. They could not see the faults in their own children regardless of how glaringly obvious they were to the rest of us.

The Hathaways' exit was a short-lived relief as they were replaced with two elderly sisters, the Misses Blake. They were kind, but slow on the uptake, and stayed significantly past thirty minutes. I snuck into the corridor after their departure and jumped into a dark room when I heard Harrison opening the front door to more visitors. Leaning against the wall, I closed my eyes, straining to hear my butler lead the guests into the drawing room. I tried to determine who they might be. The brainless variation, or otherwise.

"Why are we hiding?"

I jumped, my hand coming over my heart to slow its rapid beating. "Daniel?" I asked, unsure of who else the voice would belong to. Very little light seeped through the doorway, making the room quite dark.

"Did you not see me come in?" he asked.

I shook my head, then realized he probably could not see. The thick drapes were pulled tight, shrouding us in shadows. "No, I didn't."

"I snuck in right after you. Now tell me what is going on."

"There are more visitors," I whispered. I searched for Daniel in the dark room but could not see his form. I felt the deep rumble of his chuckle, though, and wanted to swat him, a grin forming on my lips. But judging from his voice he was a few paces out of reach.

He said, "Shall I tell them you are indisposed?"

"Heavens, no. Whatever would they think that means? I will return to the drawing room shortly. I only needed a moment to catch my breath."

"And have you caught it?"

I smiled in the darkness. "Just about."

"I will go and stall them. Take all the time you need."

"But shouldn't you be on your way to Stoneford to see your horse?" Silence filled the room. "Daniel?"

He was gone. I let out a long breath. I would only take another minute and then I would relieve him of any duty. I had meant what I said at dinner the night before. I was able to handle myself, and I did not need his help. Socially, at least. In every other respect, I was certain Corden Hall would simply be lost without him.

Only, being social was not exactly my favorite pastime. Visitors were fine, but I always ended up sitting quietly with nothing to say and the distinct feeling of tense discomfort taking over my person. It was a very physical reaction, and I did not enjoy it in the least.

It was the large groups which really got under my skin.

I took a few deep breaths and released them slowly before I let myself back into the corridor. I approached the drawing room and found Daniel sitting on the plush armchair, one ankle crossed over the other knee, his arm lazily draped over the side.

The women seated across from him on the sofa were undoubtedly related, with identical curly brown hair and steep, sloping noses. The older of the two noticed me the moment I walked through the door, her eyes raking me over in judgement before turning her attention to Daniel.

He stood as I approached, waiting to sit again until I had taken my seat in the armchair beside his.

"Allow me to introduce Miss Hurst," he said. "Miss Hurst, this is Mrs. Bennington and her daughter, Mrs. Heybourne."

"A pleasure," I said, dipping my head toward each of them. I had not heard the surname Heybourne in years, and it brought an unpleasant sensation to my gut. But this could not be a relation, surely. Not so far away from London.

The younger of the women smiled at me politely before delving back into her story. Her mother, I could plainly see, did not like me at all.

I waited for Mrs. Heybourne to complete her tale before saying, "How long have you been in the area?"

"My whole life," Mrs. Heybourne said, her smile revealing a set of deep dimples. She was pretty, but seemed rather artless. Her mother, however, had not taken her cat eyes off me since I opened my mouth.

"She is your neighbor," Daniel offered. "Just south of us at Fairlinn Court."

"Lovely." I tried to smile around the fire burning me from Mrs. Bennington's glare.

"We shall have you over for dinner!" Mrs. Heybourne exclaimed. "I should like it above all things. Most of the women in the area aren't very—"

"Matilda," Mrs. Bennington snapped, effectively silencing her daughter.

Mrs. Heybourne delicately cleared her throat, her cheeks taking on a pink tinge.

"I was riding just past your estate a few weeks back," Daniel cut in, "and saw the most extraordinary animal running down the lane. Have you acquired a new pet?"

"Oh yes, my dear Mr. Heybourne does love to indulge me. The dog is not suitable for hunting, so he belongs to me. He is called Tiny, which is an ever so clever name, for you must have seen how large he is."

"Indeed. And quite hairy."

Mrs. Heybourne grinned. "It is fun for Thomas to toss sticks and have Tiny retrieve them. He has been easy to train for all of his largeness."

"Where did you acquire him?"

She lifted her dainty shoulders. "I haven't the faintest. Mr. Heybourne knew I'd simply adore him and he brought him home for me and Thomas. Thomas did try to ride him once, but Tiny was not pleased."

I had to assume that Thomas was a child. Most likely one who belonged to Fairlinn Court.

"You must have a very kind husband," I said, trying to be sociable. I was tense already with Mrs. Bennington's unrelenting dislike, but maintained hope their visit was surely coming to a close. Whatever could I possibly have done to earn such blatant disregard?

A knock at the door sounded and Harrison stepped inside before announcing another visitor. "Miss Chappelle."

A dark-haired woman sashayed into the room, curtseying before taking the chair that I gestured for her to use.

"Miss Chappelle," Daniel said, standing. "Allow me to introduce Miss Hurst."

Miss Chappelle smiled, her red lips curving without humor. Her slanted eyes and black hair gave her the exotic look that indicated recent French ancestry.

"Such a pleasure," she said, her accent thick. Well then, not *recent* ancestry. The woman herself was French. "I didn't realize you had company, Mr. Bryce."

I turned to him sharply. I could not help my reaction. His gaze sat on the newcomer unwaveringly and he spoke at ease. "This home belongs to Miss Hurst. She has recently come to reside in it."

"Alone?" Miss Chappelle inquired, her dark eyebrow raised in question.

Mrs. Bennington gave an audible gasp. Mrs. Heybourne leaned back in her chair slightly, warily looking between Daniel and me.

"I moved into the stables the moment she arrived," Daniel said tightly. I could almost hear him finish the sentence in my mind, *not that it is any of your business.*

I was the mistress of Corden Hall, and he was my steward. There was nothing untoward about our arrangement. And regardless, I quit heeding convention the moment my father's other family was brought to light and I was discovered to be illegitimate.

This seemed enough for Mrs. Heybourne, her easy demeanor slipping back into place. Her mother, of course, reeked of distrust.

Not only did I feel the distinct need to be on my guard, but I could clearly see she did not trust *me*, either.

"What brings you to Corden Hall?" Mrs. Heybourne asked Miss Chappelle.

The French woman shot Daniel a saucy smile before answering. "I have found much to appeal to me at Corden Hall." She took a breath and continued. "The pleasure gardens to the back of the house are most diverting."

Mrs. Heybourne observed me closely. "Do you plan on remaining in Linshire permanently?"

"That shall depend," I answered. I was not about to admit that I had come here to avoid my father. "I would like to learn the details of running the estate. When that is completed, then I suppose it will depend on how I feel. I find myself relieved to be away from London at present, but I'm sure in time I shall wish to be back there."

Once my father had returned to France, of course.

"Why should you be relieved to be out of London?" Miss Chappelle asked, her voice loaded with innuendo.

I smiled at her, hoping to convey that I had nothing to hide, even though the opposite was true. "The same things that most people cite when they are glad to be free of city bounds: cleaner air, less people, more flowers."

"An astute summary," Daniel said approvingly. His posture, I noticed, had not relaxed since Miss Chappelle's arrival; he obviously felt a degree of discomfort. Was it from Mrs. Bennington's judgmental comments, Miss Chappelle's presence, or a culmination of all of the women in the room together?

I had put up with a lot this day and it was only just past noon. I was in dire need of some fresh air. And I knew just where I'd like to go as soon as these women vacated my home.

"We should be getting on," Mrs. Bennington remarked, bringing her long, thin legs to a stand. Her daughter obediently followed suit.

Mrs. Heybourne turned to Miss Chappelle. "I imagine Miss Hurst has been overrun with visitors today."

A battle of wills took place as Mrs. Heybourne and Miss Chappelle faced off. The French woman acquiesced, rising with dignified grace. She was a woman of impeccable breeding if her poise and discretion were any indication.

Goodbyes and pleasant farewells were exchanged. Mrs. Bennington halted near the door and turned. "We would love to have you to dinner soon, Miss Hurst. I eagerly await an introduction to your companion." She looked pointedly at Daniel before shifting her gaze to me. "You do have a companion, I assume."

"Of course she does," he answered smoothly. "Name the date. We would be happy to bring her to dine."

"Very good. I will consult my son-in-law and send a note forthwith."

I watched the gaggle of women exit the room with unease. I had met a variety of the ladies of Linshire over the course of the morning. While I had made some judgements myself according to their intelligence or wit, I had yet to find anyone whom I deemed a threat. But that was precisely how I categorized Mrs. Bennington and Miss Chappelle.

The daughter, Mrs. Heybourne, on the other hand, seemed perfectly friendly.

We waited in silence as Harrison showed them out, listening for the final thunk of the closing door and the click of Harrison's retreating steps.

We spoke at the same time.

"Care to explain?"

"I'm sorry—" he began.

I faced him. "You first."

"I apologize," he said. "I should not have let her goad me so. I cannot imagine how you are able to sit through visit after visit."

I raised my eyebrow. He could not change the conversation so easily.

He sighed, running a hand over his face. "It was not honest, perhaps. But I believe I have just saved your reputation."

Irrational fury ripped through me. I did not need saving. Little did he know, I did not have a reputation worth saving. "I am a confirmed spinster, Daniel. Fully fixed on the shelf. While I have acted as a companion in the past, I have never required, nor do I currently require, the consequence given by having a chaperone. I am a grown woman, and acting as my steward does not give you the right to protect me, as you see it."

His eyes glittered in suppressed irritation. "While I might not agree that you are a *confirmed* spinster, I do apologize for overstepping my bounds. You need not fear a repeat performance. I shall be in the study if you have need of me." With a curt nod, he took himself off, and I was instantly filled with regret.

I stood behind my words, but perhaps I could have delivered them with less ire.

Sinking onto the armchair behind me, I dropped my head into my hands. Navigating Linshire as the female owner of a large estate was not off to the greatest of beginnings. I needed advice, of that I was certain. Though I had just effectively burned the one bridge I had.

Coming to a stand, I tucked an errant lock of hair behind my ear and made a decision. It was time I did something about the running of this house.

CHAPTER 9

I found Mrs. Lewis with a chambermaid in the corridor, their arms full of linens.

"We are still working on a room for your cats," she said immediately. "If you can only give us a bit more time."

I flicked my hand to put away the notion. "They are fine to stay with me. They are settled now, and I doubt they would move to another room if I tried." I thought of Jasper in Aunt Georgina's home. Cats, in my experience, were territorial little creatures. And the three I brought with me to Corden Hall had all staked their claim. On my bed.

Mrs. Lewis stood rooted to the spot, blinking at me expectantly. She could at least try to make this smoother for me, could she not?

"I merely wished for a minute of your time. I would like to go over household procedures with you. And there are quite a few rooms I have found that need some sprucing up."

"I am quite busy at present," she said, eyeing the bundle of linens in her arms. The silence stretched between us until she finally continued. "But I could squeeze in a few minutes to explain the running of the house later this afternoon. Say three hours from now?"

"That will do," I said, dismissing Mrs. Lewis and the dark-haired chambermaid. I smiled at the girl and she looked uncomfortable, before bobbing a curtsy and scurrying after Mrs. Lewis.

I sighed. Someday I would have the authority and respect I deserved from my staff.

The morning parlor boasted French doors that opened onto a terrace built of the same red sandstone as the house, with marble stairs leading down to the pleasure gardens. My feet took me to the path on the left of their own accord and I found myself within the sanctuary of hedges minutes later. Sinking onto the bench, I closed my eyes and breathed in a deep, even rhythm.

I could see the wisdom of Daniel's choice, but I did not support it. Not only had he lied, but he put me into the uncomfortable position of lying as well. Whether I found a companion at once to step in and add propriety to the household or not, I would be an accomplice to his deceit.

Groaning, I reached my arms high above my head and stretched toward the sky. Hopping to my feet, I paced the small area, running the situation through my mind in hopes of finding a solution.

My thoughts continually jumped back to the moment when Miss Chappelle pointed out our lack of chaperone. Mrs. Bennington and Mrs. Heybourne were both visibly disturbed. Mr. Bryce had been correct, then. If news got out that we had been dining alone the past few days, my reputation would be ruined before I had a chance to prove myself to the people of Linshire.

I was no stranger to scandal, but in the solitude of the

enclosed garden I could admit to myself that I had looked forward to a place where no one knew of my father's indiscretions.

And there was also Daniel to think about. If nothing else, he did not deserve a soiled character because of me.

I halted, dropping my head back and squeezing my eyes closed. I did not like it one bit, but I knew what I had to do.

I took my time walking to the house, the sun warming me as I crossed the back lawn. I found the study door and paused in front of it, running the words through my mind that I needed to say. My fist was poised to knock when the door swung open and Daniel stepped out quickly, colliding with me and sending both of us to the floor.

The wind knocked out of my lungs and I struggled to breathe, the weight of a lion applying pressure on my lungs. He rolled off before helping me to stand, but it took me a moment to regain my composure. Daniel had flooded me with warmth, and my heart hammered against my breastbone.

"I apologize, Miss Hurst," he said.

I shook my head, my body still humming. "It is I who must apologize."

Daniel studied my face, his green eyes squinting in thought. He gestured to the study behind him and I stepped inside, taking a seat in a chair facing the desk. I watched him follow me in, the door left open behind him.

He surprised me, sitting in the chair beside me instead of behind the desk. He shifted to face me and waited expectantly.

I supposed I deserved that. "I am not accustomed to another person having any say in how I run my life," I said.

"Nor should that change. You are the mistress of Corden Hall."

I read nothing but sincerity in Daniel's face. It squeezed my heart when I considered how horribly I had spoken to him before. "I can see the wisdom of employing a companion.

Though to be honest, I do not know anyone who could fit the role. Unless my mother chooses to come, but I have yet to receive a reply to my last letter."

"I know of someone," he said quietly, glancing away. He looked back, holding my gaze, his eyes unsure. "I do not wish to cause any discomfort, but if you are agreeable to the idea, I can have her here within four days."

Who was this woman that could drop her life in four days and move to another house? Daniel had already admitted he had no family.

"It would not be permanent," I ventured cautiously. "I am not even sure *I* am a permanent fixture at Corden Hall, so I do not want to set up false expectations of fixed employment."

Daniel's gaze grew thoughtful, his green eyes clear. "Is any employment truly fixed?"

A small smile graced my lips. "I suppose not."

We sat in silence, my mind working through the emotions of the day while trying to read Daniel's expression. It had been trying, to say the least, and he looked just as exhausted as I felt. Which was unfair. He'd sat through one visit. I had sat through significantly more.

"Are you decided?" he asked.

I sighed. What choice did I have? There was no sense in further ruining my reputation for the sake of my pride. "Yes. You may write to her."

"I will do you one better, ma'am, and I shall retrieve her myself."

"Oh," I said, stunned. "Is she nearby?"

His smile was full of concealed amusement and he glanced away, leaning back in his chair as he stretched his arms high above his head, much like I had done in the garden earlier. Daniel must have had a measure of pent-up frustration as well, and I was glad we were finding a way back to our easy companionship. We were not quite there, but we were closer.

"I must pack right away." He stood to go. "It would be a good idea to get on the road as soon as possible."

"Daniel?" I asked when he reached the doorway.

He turned to me, his handsome face a picture of calm inquiry.

"Thank you."

He smiled, his dimple making an appearance and causing my stomach to flip. He bowed to me and turned to go, and I watched him as far as the corridor before he stepped from my sight.

I could not deny the pull I felt toward him, nor the feelings he kindled within me. I was not prepared for either of those things, and it terrified me. The trip to retrieve this mystery companion was superbly timed. My heart could do with a few days away from Daniel to regulate itself.

For I could *not* afford to fall in love.

"Ma'am?"

I jerked my head away from the window, the cloud of dust left behind by Daniel's traveling carriage beginning to fall and settle. "Hmm?"

Mrs. Lewis clasped her hands in her lap, her face a picture of poorly disguised irritation. "I simply wondered what you were hoping to accomplish from this meeting so that I might be able to focus my instruction."

"Yes, thank you. That is wise."

She sat across from me on a parlor chair in the drawing room, a small writing table between us. We were situated beside the long front windows and had a clear view of the driveway. I had been able to watch Daniel's case get loaded onto the boot of the vehicle and his graceful climb inside. His head had turned slightly before he got in, but I wasn't sure if he'd seen me through the window or was merely looking back at the house. But, alas, there was no sign on his face to indicate recognition. I hoped he was not still upset about our earlier conflict.

"Do you have a list, perhaps?" Mrs. Lewis prodded, bringing me from my reverie again.

"I apologize, Mrs. Lewis. It appears my mind cannot settle." I took in a breath, lifting my posture, and redirected my thoughts to the task at hand. "I do not have a list, no. I would like to know everything about the running of the house. And I would like to understand why the upper floor has gone into disrepair."

Her eyes widened and I noticed they were a lovely shade of brown. Her white hair was drawn back into a tight knot at the base of her neck, and it occurred to me that I had thought her older than she likely was. She must have been a fair blonde in her youth.

I continued, "I can see how the task may seem daunting, but I would like to invest myself in the running of this house. I am not sure where my life will lead me, but I should like to remain here for the present and would appreciate it if we could find a way to live in harmony." I inserted a healthy dose of forthright weight into my words. I wanted her to know I could tell she was not pleased with me and I hoped for that to change. As the housekeeper, Mrs. Lewis and I would be working hand in hand and it would benefit the entire household if we had a harmonious relationship.

She regarded me thoughtfully before clearing her throat. "The maids have a schedule they keep to and I can run you through it at a later time. For now, let us walk through the house, perhaps? I can give you a detailed tour and you may point out what areas you'd like to improve."

I stood. "That sounds wonderful." She could help me fill in the gaps from my own misguided snooping.

"We shall begin in the kitchen."

I followed Mrs. Lewis downstairs, weaving through servants

as she showed me the essential rooms in the kitchen area. The stillroom, polishing room, her own private parlor, and the butler's room.

She gestured to Harrison's domain. "That used to be the steward's office, but Mr. Bryce found he could meet with gentlemen farmers easier upstairs and moved all of his things into the study. It wasn't being used at the time so no one argued with him."

They wouldn't though, anyway, would they? Not when he outranked the butler. Besides, raised as a gentleman, it must have been difficult for Daniel to come and reside in a large manor house and run the entire place from a small, dark office underground. I could not fault his decision at all. But then, I was not a servant.

"Harrison did not find it presumptuous?" I asked.

"No," she answered, leading me back up the servants' stairs. "He had no reason to complain, anyway."

We mounted the steps in silence, reaching a room at the top lined with counters and cupboards. "The linens are kept here."

And the serving dishes, I assumed, before they were brought to the dining room.

We stepped through the door into the corridor and Mrs. Lewis took me through each of the main rooms, describing which days they were cleaned and the general duties of the maids in each of the rooms. We ended at the morning parlor, coming full circle, and she proceeded to lead me outside and explain the upkeep of the pleasure gardens and the list of gardeners responsible for their maintenance.

"Have they always been so well maintained?" I asked.

"Yes," she replied simply. "They were the pride of your grandmother's heart, and when the estate fell from her hands and no one came to claim it, we simply proceeded forth as we always had before. There was no one telling us to stop their upkeep, so we did not. It would have felt a large disservice to the missus to allow her precious garden to fall into disrepair."

It struck me how lonely Corden Hall must have felt for the last twenty years living without a master or mistress in residence. It would have become second nature to the servants to speak to and treat the steward as though he were in charge, for *someone* needed to be, and he was the man calling the shots. The only correspondence I had ever had with members of Corden Hall's household had been with the stewards. The same was true, I believed, for my father before I had taken control.

In that line of thought, the only direction Mrs. Lewis, Harrison, or any of the servants had received, came from Daniel. Or Mr. Aiken before him.

"I have been derelict in my duties," I said quietly, realizing the burden I had placed on Daniel's shoulders by remaining away. I turned to Mrs. Lewis. "I apologize for my neglect. It was callous and thoughtless."

I seemed to have startled her. Her brown eyes widened, and she glanced away, clearly uncomfortable with my directness. Anyone would feel a sense of protection and loyalty toward their home when a new person stepped forward and took control. It was likely why Perkins, Aunt Georgina's butler, disliked me. He could not have appreciated my taking control over the house when it did not belong to me, but to Elsie. Mrs. Lewis had likely felt bothered by my sudden appearance and control. She had been the woman in charge for twenty years and I suddenly stepped in to take over.

"I can see now how much work you do," I said, doing my best to sound sincere, "and I am prepared to lighten your burden. I should like to work together to restore Corden Hall to its former glory. I have ignored the estate for far too long."

"You were a child when your grandmother passed," she said kindly.

"But I've been an independent woman for these last four

years. I have had plenty of time to rectify the situation and no great reason not to."

"That is in the past," Mrs. Lewis said, her flat lips forming the semblance of a smile for the first time. "You cannot change that. You can only do better moving forward."

CHAPTER 10

The following day was an overwhelming experiment in tolerance. Mrs. Lewis instructed me on the various aspects of the running of the house in between calls from more neighbors and interested townsfolk.

It had become clear by the second callers that word had gotten around town about my sudden occupation at Corden Hall without a chaperone. Daniel's absence added credence to the general assumption that he had gone to retrieve a companion for me, and without even knowing her name, I was unable to dispute the pointed questions.

As thinly veiled speculations shot at me from various callers, I deflected as best I could, merely explaining that Daniel had provided me with a chaperone, but I was still growing used to the woman. He, on the other hand, had a preexisting relationship with her and it was not strange at all that he had requested her services on his latest business trip. Reason prevailed that if Daniel was not in residence then my need for a companion departed with him.

It was apparent that I was stalling for time, but I held on to hope that the people of Linshire would lend me a measure of compassion and take my words at face value. So far, I had not been greatly disappointed.

Mr. Bowen, the gentleman farmer from the other side of town, did not seem to care why Daniel had left or where he was. He was simply disappointed to have lost a conversation partner. "I wanted to inquire on his opinions of my latest acquisition," he said rather moodily. He reminded me much of a plump child disappointed he did not get an extra sweet at teatime.

"I apologize for the inconvenience, sir," I said. "He would no doubt love to discuss your horse had he been here."

Mr. Bowen harrumphed, sitting back in his chair. His wife, a very similar, only smaller, version of her husband, smiled kindly. "I had wondered if he was gone. I saw his carriage driving south just last evening and thought to myself, he cannot be coming home this very night, surely. He must be gone for at least a day."

"How very astute you are."

She dipped her head coyly. "You are kind, Miss Hurst. I am so very glad you've come to Linshire."

The sincerity lacing her words was not quite unprecedented, exactly, but perhaps the closest thing I had come to an authentic person since beginning visits the day prior. I found that I liked this woman very much.

She leaned forward as though she was going to impart a secret. "And I've got a special surprise for you if you would indulge me."

I tried to hide my unease. It could not be good if I was meant to indulge her. "Oh?"

"We would love to have you for dinner tomorrow evening if you think it should suit? I can send my carriage for you, since Mr. Bryce has taken yours."

"I am afraid my companion is unavailable at present, as well."

"That is no matter," she said dismissively, flapping her hand. "Mr. Bowen and I would serve just fine."

She continued to lean forward as she awaited my answer. She was only thinly veiling her anticipation, and I found I could not disappoint the woman.

"I would like that very much."

Clapping gleefully, she roused Mr. Bowen from his examination of Mrs. Covey's ginger biscuits.

"We will send the carriage at half past five."

"I shall be ready," I said, smiling. Mrs. Bowen's enthusiasm was infectious, and I looked forward to the dinner despite my initial reservations.

The Bowens stood to leave, and I walked them out to the corridor, nodding as Mrs. Bowen jabbered on about Corden Hall's magnificence and how it simply *begged* to house a ball. The hint was not subtle in the least.

"We shall see you tomorrow!" she called as she walked outside. My smile stretched as I raised a hand to wave them away.

I returned to the drawing room and sank onto the sofa. Picking up a ginger biscuit, I closed my eyes and enjoyed the moist, dark sugar melting on my tongue. I had been afraid Mr. Bowen would eat them all before I had the opportunity to try one. And lucky me, he had saved me two.

What was the general etiquette on denying callers in the country? It had been so long since I lived away from London that I could not recall what my mother would do when unwanted guests arrived. In London I was never bothered by turning people from the door, but here we were not in close proximity to our neighbors. Anyone hoping for a visit had to travel at least some distance.

I considered the situation from my mother's point of view, but it was not entirely helpful. She was such a kind, bubbly person that she never had cause to reject a friend. She welcomed everyone equally into her home. At least, she had when she'd had a home of her own.

It was strange that she had no desire to return to Corden Hall. She did not grow up here, entirely, but she had spent a decent amount of time in this house between all of the estates her father had owned and operated.

But I had written her right away when I decided to move to Linshire and she expressed her contentment in remaining with her sister's family quite clearly. Even the renewal of my invitation was unlikely to receive a favorable response.

Hoofbeats sounded in the drive and I stood at once, crossing to the windows and peeking behind the curtain to get a glimpse at the next visitors. I gasped when my eyes fell on the familiar carriage. Dropping the curtain, I lifted my hem and ran for the front door.

"Elsie!" I called, rushing past Harrison with unladylike haste. "What are you doing here?"

She looked up as her husband helped her step onto the gravel drive. Her clothes were crumpled from the trip and her eyes tired. "I missed you," she said, coming to embrace me.

I stepped back, taking in her clear exhaustion, and that of her husband. I had made the trip myself only the week prior. It was not all that tiring, to be honest. Worry blossomed in my chest and I tried to tamp it back down until I had just cause.

"I hope we are not intruding?" Lord Cameron said.

"You are always welcome," I responded immediately. "I am delighted, but surprised."

"I am afraid it will not be a long visit," he said regretfully, following us into the house. "We are visiting a few estates north of here and Elsie insisted on coming to see you on our way through."

"I am so glad you did." I led them into the foyer. "Harrison, please ask Mrs. Lewis to have a room prepared for my friends."

He bowed and walked away as the footmen carried their trunks inside. "How long shall I have you here?" I asked.

"Two days," Lord Cameron replied instantly. "We must keep our appointments or my man of business will have my head." A grin belied the severity of his words, but I could appreciate the importance of keeping an appointment all the same.

I asked a passing maid to have a fresh pot of tea sent to the drawing room. "And refresh the tray of biscuits, if Mrs. Covey has any to spare."

"Yes, ma'am."

I led the Nichols into the drawing room and gestured for them to sit.

"I should change first," Elsie said, eyeing the cream sofa.

"Whatever you prefer." I grinned. "I am just so glad to see you."

By the time Elsie and Lord Cameron had changed and returned to the drawing room the tea had been replenished and a fresh plate of still warm ginger cookies adorned the tray. I began pouring as the couple took their seats on the cream sofa. It was evident Elsie had needed the restoring element of washing up, for she looked a great deal more awake.

"I cannot wait to meet this steward you spoke so highly of," Lord Cameron commented, accepting a hot cup of tea.

"I'm afraid you shall probably miss him," I said regretfully. "He is away fetching me a companion and is due to arrive in three days' time."

Elsie's cup sat suspended before her open mouth. "Whatever are you talking about?"

"I need a companion to lend me consequence. I must protect my reputation—and that of my steward's—by placing a virtuous woman in the house."

"You are a virtuous woman," she said, a bit defensively. "I cannot recall the last time you cared to have a chaperone. *You've acted the companion for the last few years.*"

I placed my cup on the table beside my chair and picked up another ginger biscuit. They were particularly addicting, I was coming to realize. "Word has gotten out that I have come to reside in Corden Hall, and I've been receiving visits from every woman in the parish. It has been quite eye opening to the expectations the people of Linshire hold, and I found that it was simply more comfortable to agree to a companion than to try and prove my independence."

"What do you know about this companion?"

I shrugged. "Nothing, really. But I trust Mr. Bryce's judgment."

Elsie's eyebrows hitched up. "You must really value his discretion if you are allowing him to choose a companion for you."

"He has yet to prove me wrong."

"Now I am tempted to let Cameron go see the estates for himself and remain behind. I would really like to meet this companion and make a decision for myself how well Mr. Bryce can judge what a woman needs."

Lord Cameron gave his wife a look. "You are expecting a hag?"

"It matters not what she looks like, but whether she values discretion. Does she know when to step in, and when to make herself scarce?"

"Elsie!" I reprimanded. "This woman will not be a servant."

"Nor do I think she must be treated as one. I only imply that, as a companion, she is meant to lend consequence to the household, and there will be times when you, Freya, will need time to yourself." She eyed me knowingly and I realized how very valid her point was. I valued my privacy and time to myself very highly.

I was not in the habit of having my every move noted or even cared about. As my companion, that would be her job. I dropped my head into my hands, rubbing the sockets of my eyes. I had to remind myself that there was a very valid purpose in hiring a companion. It was necessary at this juncture in my life; it would not be necessary forever.

"It is merely a formality," I finally said, lifting my head. "And I made it clear before Daniel left that I would not need her permanently, for I don't even know how long I am to remain at Corden Hall. We simply need to guard our reputations."

Elsie sat frozen, her eyes unblinking. Lord Cameron looked between his wife and me, as lost as I was as to why she was so bothered.

"Elsie?" he asked. "What is it?"

"Nothing," she answered, snapping out of her strange mood and giving him a sweet smile. "I only feel like I should decide for myself if this companion is a worthy hire. And meeting this Mr. Bryce—or Daniel, was it?—would be an added bonus."

I quickly thought back over my words. Had I referred to him by his given name? I was rather sure I hadn't. I had been so careful to think of Daniel as Mr. Bryce when Elsie came in. Could I have slipped?

"We cannot leave Mr. Sweeney waiting, love," Lord Cameron said apologetically. "He is showing us three estates and has them all planned out with the owners meticulously. It is a great favor to me and I cannot ask him to reschedule."

Elsie frowned. "I know this. I only wish it wasn't so."

I found myself increasingly grateful that it *was* so. With Elsie's astute observations, it was clear she was reading deeply into the situation. Deeper than it warranted, of course, but it was important that she did not begin having expectations which were both unnecessary and illogical.

I was really not doing well on my resolve to think of Daniel less as he was away. In fact, I was beginning to see that I was thinking of him more and more.

"I have an idea," I said. "I need to write a neighbor of mine and beg off of a dinner she invited me to. Why don't we all go for a ride when I am finished, and I can show you around the estate?"

"Splendid," Lord Cameron said.

"May I snoop around your house in the time being?" Elsie inquired.

"Snoop away."

CHAPTER 11

"And that wood over there marks the property line." I pointed. "I own the area that curves, but the trees off to the left belong to the owners of Fairlinn Court."

Elsie scanned the horizon. "You have a significant area of land. I am suitably impressed."

"I, as well," Lord Cameron said.

I swept my gaze over the fields behind us and the woods to my right. "I did not know before I came how fortunate I am," I agreed.

"Have you met your neighbors yet?"

"Of Fairlinn Court?" I recalled the conversation that led to my argument with Daniel. Mrs. Bennington and her superior ways were no match for Miss Chappelle and her saucy smiles, sending eyes to Daniel with everything she said. Fire burned through my chest at the memory, but I shook it off. "Yes. Mrs. Heybourne was lovely."

Elsie glanced at me quickly. "Is she any relation to the Major? I have not seen him since our first Season."

"I did not ask," I said. In truth, it had not occurred to me to do so. "Surely it is a common name."

"Perhaps they are cousins," Elsie said, musing. "Did he have a sister?"

Yes, he did. But that was hardly relevant. I said, "She is married to a Heybourne. Her mother is a Bennington."

Elsie's determined brow made her look like Rosalynn. It was not a look I appreciated. "We must find out. Shall we ride over and visit now?"

Could Elsie not see how that might be uncomfortable for me? I turned my horse toward home and my guests quickly followed suit.

"Perhaps dropping in unannounced would not be very polite," Lord Cameron said. "We are here to see Miss Hurst, Elsie, not to step into her life and begin playing with it as though it was a game of chess."

She was affronted. "I am no meddler!"

Lord Cameron's face said otherwise.

"You are reminding me a great deal of Rosalynn," I said, trying to keep a straight face. I knew the comparison would bother her. She would not like to have it pointed out that she tended to mother me, either. It was entirely possible, though, that she did not realize she did it.

"Who is up for a race back to the stables?" Elsie asked.

"You're on," her husband said, kicking his horse in the side.

They sped off at once, and I watched them go. I was happy Elsie had found Lord Cameron. I only wished that her love for her husband did not blind her to my contentedness. It was acceptable for us to have different paths in life, both full of our own kind of happiness.

I entered the stable some little time later to find Lord Cameron and Elsie already dismounted and waiting inside.

"You have a fantastic selection of horses here," Lord Cameron said as I slipped down from my mount.

"Most of them belong to Mr. Bryce," I explained, lifting the hem of my skirt from the mud and tossing it over my arm. "He is dabbling in horse breeding."

Lord Cameron's eyebrows shot up. "Is he? Now I am even tempted to remain behind a day or two. I should like to question the man, if I am being truthful. I've heard he has some fine blood here."

"I will tell him you said so," I said, turning for the house. "There is likely no greater compliment you could possibly pay the man than that." Elsie and Lord Cameron fell into step beside me.

"You allow your steward quite a bit of freedom," Elsie remarked. "It is rather unprecedented, is it not?"

I shrugged, my gaze on the rear of the house. "I am not sure. I do not have excessive experience in managing a steward or an estate. But Mr. Bryce has done a wonderful job this last year and he did ask me about the horses when I hired him on. He pays a boarding fee and covers the cost of their feed, so it is really none of my concern so long as I have room for my own animals and Mr. Bryce continues to do the job I pay him to do."

"That is generous of you, nonetheless," Lord Cameron said.

My cheeks warmed at the praise. It was not as though I had actually done anything for Daniel. I simply allowed him to do it himself. It was an odd thing to be praised for and I swallowed my discomfort.

"Tell me about Rosalynn," I said, deflecting the attention from myself.

"She is well," Elsie said at once. "Her child is growing quickly, according to her doctor. And the boys are all healthy."

"She wishes for a girl, does she not?"

Elsie shot me a knowing look. "She won't say as much out loud, but I am sure she does. She quit talking about genders when the last twins were born."

"Poor Rosie. She just wants to dress up a little girl..."

Elsie added, "And put ribbons in her hair..."

"And lovely little coats and tiny shoes."

I grinned, imagining a tiny Rosalynn and how darling she would be. I glanced at Elsie and the look of longing on her face caused my stomach to drop. This could not be a happy topic of conversation for her.

We went into the house and I left them at the top of the stairs. "I suppose we ought to change for dinner. I shall see you downstairs?"

Elsie nodded and Lord Cameron led her away after shooting me a commiserating smile. It could not be easy for him to watch his beloved suffer.

Tilly was waiting for me when I entered my bedchamber. We proceeded with changing for dinner and washing away the dirt and stench of horses in silence. We had an easy rhythm between us, and I was grateful she was not a chatterbox. I valued quiet, thoughtful time for reflection.

The Nichols were already in the drawing room by the time I made it downstairs. Elsie seemed quiet and withdrawn, the smile she tried to give me an obvious effort. I wished I could ask her about her troubles, but it was not my place. It was obviously a personal struggle, and if she felt I would be a valuable confidant, then she would have to open that door of conversation on her own.

I simply had to convince myself that her husband was sufficient support and let it go.

Elsie found me in the morning parlor, the sun streaming through the French doors and warming the sofa where I sat, Cleo nestled beside me. "We are planning to leave quite early in the morning," she said. "Cameron is having our things packed and we will say our farewells this evening. How shall we spend our day?"

"I have been considering a trip into Linshire," I said. "Or we could walk to the brook. Tilly informed me there is a lovely stream that runs through the woods and makes for a nice afternoon walk. I've yet to see it though, so with me leading the group, we take with us the potential to get lost."

"Part of the fun, I'd say," Lord Cameron said, gliding into the room.

"I find I would like to see Linshire." Elsie grinned. "It might be useful to see what sort of shops the little town has to offer."

"Useful for whom?" Lord Cameron asked, his eyebrow raised as he stood over his wife's chair.

"Freya, of course. Unless *we* found an estate nearby."

Lord Cameron seated himself, letting out a long, drawn-out breath. "I would not be opposed to it, of course, but it is unrealistic. My man of business put together a comprehensive list of available estates that contained every one of our demands and there was nothing in Shropshire."

Elsie sighed. "Do not fear, for I shall not pout. But let us explore Linshire anyway."

I stood, forcing Cleo to jump from the sofa and scamper out the door. "I'll call for the carriage."

We found ourselves amidst the bustling main street in Linshire with more people than I had expected. A steady flow of foot traffic lined the streets, and Elsie and I took our time moving between the shops, admiring bonnets and filling our reticules with sweets.

"I am sorry to leave you so soon," Elsie said, popping a peppermint into her mouth. Her eyes followed me often through the day and melancholy seemed to seep from her, but I still could not place its cause. While I wanted to sympathize with her, it was impossible when she would not admit me into her confidence.

"You may quit watching me that way," I finally said, more harshly than I intended.

She reared back slightly, her eyes growing wide.

I pulled her away from the front door of the milliner's shop and down the walk. "I am sorry, I should not have snapped. But it is difficult to think when you are throwing your sad eyes my way so consistently." The temptation to ask what troubled her sat on me like a cat preparing to pounce, but I could not bring myself to say anything. I was not like Elsie. I could not confront others, regardless of how compelled I felt. I needed her to come to me.

"I did not realize," she breathed. "I suppose I ought to tell you, but I had wished it wouldn't come to this."

"Then do not. I would rather not be a burden. You need not struggle further by rehashing your troubles in the middle of the street."

She looked taken aback at once. "But they are not my troubles, Freya, it is—"

She was cut off at once by a loud voice bellowing across the street. "Do my eyes deceive me?"

We turned in unison, and I found myself rooted to the spot as the man I did not want to see crossed through traffic, his jovial face a picture of delight—quite the opposite of what I was feeling.

"Major Heybourne!" Elsie stepped forward, giving him her hand. "I wondered if you had a relation nearby when Freya mentioned meeting a Mrs. Heybourne recently. I had not believed we would be so lucky to see you once again. It has been many years, has it not?"

"Yes, indeed," he responded, his eyes swinging to land on my own. "But I am afraid it is just Mr. Heybourne, now."

"I am not sure I will ever be able to think of you as a mister," Elsie said.

I dipped my head at once in a curtsy, postponing the need for conversation by every beat of the clock that I could. It was odd to see the man who had once so passionately begged for my hand in marriage, regardless of how long ago it had occurred. I found my cheeks heating at the memory and I looked away, begging silently for the uncomfortable reunion to come to a hasty end.

"And the Mrs. Heybourne of Fairlinn Court," Elsie inquired, her eyes lit up. "Is she a close relation?"

"My wife," he answered, his smile growing.

An odd sense of relief filtered through me. I made purposeful eye contact and tried to smile, Mr. Heybourne's easy congeniality setting me at ease. There were no unfavorable feelings on his end, so far as I could tell.

"I liked her very much," I said, as though my opinion carried any weight. I instantly regretted my words. Was I trying to show him that he had, indeed, made the better choice? To reinforce my avid refusal from years before? Warmth bled up my neck and filled my cheeks. The gall of it, really.

The Major, however, seemed inclined to look past my folly. "She returns the sentiment, Miss Hurst. She had nothing but kind words to say on her return home from your visit."

"Naturally." Elsie laughed.

"We would love to have you to dinner," he replied, swinging his gaze between us. "Both of you. Can we schedule an evening next week?"

Elsie's pout was very real. Lord Cameron came to stand behind her as she said, "I am afraid I leave in the morning. I would have loved to make the acquaintance of your wife."

The men exchanged hearty greetings before we said our farewells and parted ways. It appeared Mr. Heybourne did not have a single bitter bone in his body. He was a saint, probably incapable of resentful thoughts. Though he had every right to despise me, I was glad he did not. Or, if he did, he hid it well.

We completed our shopping and made our way back to the estate, but I could not remove the encounter from my mind. Elsie was unaware that the Major proposed during our social

Season years before. The event had been embarrassing and awkward, and I had succeeded in avoiding the man ever since.

One thought continued to present itself, and I could not shake it. I had kept the ordeal a secret, but had he? Or had Mr. Heybourne told his wife about our unfortunate past?

CHAPTER 12

Initially, Mrs. Overton was not the sort of woman I would peg for a companion. She was small, almost fragile-looking in both appearance and demeanor. Her gray hair was styled into a loose bun at the nape of her neck that complimented her soft features and added to the overall effect that she was delicate.

When Daniel led her into the drawing room and seated her on the sofa across from me, I felt immediate concern for her ability to complete her task. When she caught my eye and smiled though, I was instantly won over by her earnest gaze and intelligent bearing. She was, it seemed to me, a woman of advancing years that once held—and perhaps still possessed—a considerable measure of fire. Whether she was fiercely loyal, or simply steadfast and dependable, it was clear I could trust her.

"Thank you for stepping in with such haste," I said. "It could not have been convenient for you."

She looked to Daniel and affection filled her countenance, wrinkling the corners of her eyes and pulling at the edges of her lips. She had come for him; it was not even a question.

Daniel smiled back at the woman before directing his grin at me. "I think you will find that Mrs. Overton is particularly obliging. We had best not take too much advantage of her."

She leaned over and picked up Daniel's hand in her own, squeezing once. "Impossible."

There was certainly more here than met the eye. I was prepared to inquire on their relationship when Daniel stood, effectively cutting me off. "Mrs. Lewis has prepared a bedchamber on the same floor as Miss Hurst. I will show you there directly if you would like, Mrs. Overton, and then we can return in time for dinner."

She stood and followed him from the room, leaving me with a cold teapot and sadly darkening windows. Melancholy settled on my shoulders and they stooped accordingly. I wanted to follow Daniel's warmth from the room but instead remained seated, my mind drifting to the events of the previous few days.

Elsie hadn't confided in me before they departed. She had been so close, but Mr. Heybourne's appearance ceased all talk at once. I could only assume that her trouble was related to her lack of children. Perhaps my own naivety had a role to play, but four years of marriage with no children seemed cause enough to come to terms with the sad truth that she would not become a mother. Rosalynn's pregnancies could not make that any easier to bear.

"You look as though you've got the weight of a thousand worlds on your shoulders."

I looked up to catch Daniel's compassionate gaze regarding me.

"I received a visit from a friend while you were gone," I explained. "Her worries have become my own. I wish it were within my power to do more for her, but I am afraid no earthly being could extinguish her troubles completely."

A furrow appeared in his brow and he crossed into the room, his damp hair and immaculate clothing a testament that he'd been in his chambers for quite some time. I had really lost myself to pondering.

"Regardless of your inability to help, in your opinion, it is a noble notion to wish it, and your friend is fortunate indeed to have you by her side."

My mouth broke into a semblance of a smile. "It is enough to wish to help? Dear me, I've been going about it wrong all these years."

"Do not misread my words," he said, his smile deepening. "I only meant—well, I believe you know precisely what I meant."

"I believe I do." I glanced away, his steady gaze too much to hold. "I like Mrs. Overton," I offered.

His smile turned pensive. "You were correct earlier. It cost her greatly to come. I believe, however, it is for the best, regardless of what *she* believes at present."

His words could not have sounded any more mysterious had he *tried* to make them so.

Mrs. Overton arrived shortly after and we made our way into the dining room. I took the head of the table, flanked by Daniel and my new companion. Conversation flowed neatly, topics ranging from the weather to the local parishioners and various updates on their lives. Mrs. Overton possessed a decent understanding of the people in the area, though she admitted it was her first time to Linshire. I could only come to the conclusion that Daniel had written to her, and frequently, by the sound of it.

"I have it in my mind to restore the bedchambers," I said. "There seems to be only one usable guest room and it was recently inhabited by yourself."

Daniel nodded, finishing a bite of potatoes. "It did not appear that way when I first arrived."

"Tell me something," I requested, lowering my fork and leaning closer. "Why have the servants taken great pains to keep up the gardens, but the interior of the house has been left to deteriorate? Is the structure of the building in any sort of danger?" I had noticed a few cracks lining the wall in the morning parlor earlier, and it worried me.

"The building is solid. I can only assume that Mr. Aiken or your father did not sign off on the purchases required to keep up the rooms."

"Then I shall," I said. "What say you, Mrs. Overton? Shall we restore this home to a state of respectability?"

"I am not sure I am the right person for the job," she said. "I cannot do much more than sit and point."

"We'll need someone to point," Daniel said quickly. "There must be a person in charge of making sure we are putting things right."

I glanced between Daniel and Mrs. Overton as they shared a sweet smile. The nature of their relationship was a mystery. They were not forthcoming with information about it, and if I was not mistaken, Daniel even went so far as to intentionally avoid the topic.

But I was not about to employ a companion when I did not know her full story.

I steeled my resolve. I would have to be careful, but I was going to get to the bottom of this one way or another.

The morning room had undoubtedly become my favorite room in the house. Not only did it possess a clear view of the pleasure gardens, but it was light, warm, and comfortable in the mornings. And it had been very well maintained.

Mrs. Overton joined Coco and me there shortly after breakfast.

"Where do you come from, Miss Hurst?" she asked, her hands clasped lightly in her lap, an easy smile on her mouth.

"I have been in London the last four years. I grew up in the countryside, but I cannot seem to remember much of it. Town life has consumed the majority of my adult years."

"I never liked London much." She shook her head slowly, her mouth turned down in distaste. "It was too busy and the air too thick."

I smiled indulgently. "That is a common complaint, to be sure. Where do you hail from, Mrs. Overton?" It was a natural progression of the conversation, yet I still felt nervous. I had the feeling that Daniel did not want me to pry.

"A beautiful little town called Hannoville outside of London. Though far enough away to be called country. Have you been there?"

"I can't say that I have. It does not sound familiar."

She nodded as though she expected that answer.

"It is very small, but I loved it. We had the sort of community that loved and supported one another. My neighbors were people I've known most of my life."

I stilled. How selfish I felt. One word of acceptance from me and Daniel sped off to steal this kind woman from a home she'd known her entire life? "You needn't remain at Corden Hall," I said cautiously. "I am sure we can find another companion if you'd like to return to your home."

Mrs. Overton gazed fondly out the window. It was unclear whether her gaze landed on the gardens or reached some far away dream. "I am content, dear. Do not fret."

That was an easy request, but difficult in execution. "Very well."

Harrison entered the room, proffering a letter on a silver tray. I took the note and sliced the wax seal with a knife before setting it back on the tray. The handwriting was foreign to me, and the seal unfamiliar as well.

"Oh," I said aloud, surprised to read the content of the letter. "Mrs. Heybourne has invited us to dine tomorrow night. She is our neighbor of Fairlinn Court. She would love to meet you." I glanced up at Mrs. Overton, her face a picture of quiet contentment. "If you are agreeable."

"I am at your disposal," she replied, her tone void of malice. She was, it appeared, entirely comfortable being at my disposal.

It was an altogether foreign feeling.

I understood that she was a paid member of the household. Someone there to do my bidding, stay with me always, and lend me a certain level of virtue. I was a companion to Aunt Georgina for almost four years, though in a blessed circumstance, and did not truly live the sorry life a paid companion typically endured. How was I to convey to this woman that she was capable of making her own choices, that she need not cater to me? I had been independent ever since the scandal broke free and my mother fled London. I did not need a motherly figure then, and I certainly didn't now.

I stood, Coco at my heels, and Mrs. Overton followed suit.

"I have a meeting with Mrs. Lewis. I shall see you afterward."

I could tell I'd surprised the woman, but I did not wait around to see what she had to say. I spun on my heel and made my way toward the servant staircase that led down to the kitchens. I was going to find Mrs. Lewis and she was going to teach me something.

I caught Daniel's retreating form in the corridor and called out to him. He glanced over his shoulder and my stomach did a flip. It was not unpleasant, and caused my breathing to come in quicker takes. Dratted *feelings*. They would go away, eventually. They always did.

"We've received an invitation to dine at Fairlinn Court tomorrow evening," I said, fiddling with my skirts between my fingertips. Coco came around my feet and began sniffing at Daniel's shoes.

"That will be nice. I've always liked Mr. Heybourne."

I felt unaccountably irritated. "Yes, most people do. Shall I give an acceptance for the household?"

He peered at me closely, his eyebrows pulling together slightly. "Are you certain I am invited?"

"Yes, Mrs. Heybourne mentioned you by name. I feel like I will need your support, if you are willing to lend it."

He moved as though to step closer but paused, his face fixed on my own. "Always, Freya. That is what I am here for."

I found myself lost within his gaze until he pulled me straight out again. The romantic within me that had begun to make an appearance was firmly put in her place. Daniel chose to be here, yes, but he was also being paid for it.

He worked for me.

I had to get away.

Turning on my heel, I made my way back into the morning room, past Mrs. Overton where she remained on the couch, and through the French doors. I took a left where the path forked, vaguely aware of Coco following behind me, and let myself into the hedge-protected fortress, falling onto the bench and breathing rapidly. I was setting up expectations I had no business creating, and I was going to be let down. I needed to harden the wall around my heart. And I needed to do it thoroughly.

CHAPTER 13

"Shall we begin?" I said, finishing my tea and setting the cup on the tray.

Mrs. Overton glanced up from her tea. She wasn't nearly finished, and I swallowed my urgency. There was no rush to fix up the house, of course. Daniel had said himself the walls were sturdy. The morning room itself only needed new paint. But the undertaking would give me ample purpose and an excuse to spend hours upstairs. An added benefit when I was doing my utmost to install distance between my steward and myself. I liked the man, of course, but that was the problem. Filling my mind with wallpaper and new furniture would leave little room to think of Daniel, surely.

"I suppose we can wait a few more minutes. I am only eager to begin," I explained.

"Begin what, dear?" she asked softly.

"Fixing up the guest bedrooms. I am sure there are more areas of the house which need attention but I feel we should start there. The whole floor above my bedchamber is in disrepair."

She set her cup down and pulled herself to stand. "Let us go."

We made our way to the correct floor and decided to check each room together and determine where to begin. By the time we reached the other end of the corridor I had a list so long of things to acquire that I wondered at the wisdom of this project. Surely I did not have sufficient need to house quite so many people in my guest rooms. Perhaps if we chose one or two rooms to get us started, the rest would occur in time.

"This is quite the undertaking," Mrs. Overton said as we stood in the bedroom at the far end of the corridor. The wallpaper was peeling and the fireplace was particularly dirty. A bed sat in the center of the far wall, but the flimsy design had fallen to the floor the moment I rested on its edge, billowing a cloud of dust. I could only be grateful it was I and not Mrs. Overton who had taken that fated seat. "This sort of neglect takes years to achieve. It had to have begun before your grandmother's time."

"I can only imagine that she hadn't seen the need." I shrugged, trying to avoid rubbing my rear end where I'd fallen from the bed frame and landed on the floor. "I did not know her."

"Shall we return downstairs and begin a list?"

I followed her from the room. We installed ourselves in the morning room once again and Mrs. Overton pulled the bell.

"It is such a shame the house is not fit for company. This task is perhaps too large an undertaking, but I would like to do my best to restore it."

The dark-haired maid came in and stood, waiting expectantly.

"I gave Mrs. Lewis my particular tea blend," Mrs. Overton said. "I should like some now."

"Yes, ma'am."

She turned away, and I waited for Mrs. Overton to explain

herself, but the room remained silent as she picked up her sewing basket instead and pulled a length of cloth from it.

I pulled my own basket from beneath the sofa and picked up an embroidery I was nearly finished with. When the maid returned with the tea, I awaited Mrs. Overton's polite offer to share, but she did not satisfy my curiosity. I watched her a moment. Would it be uncouth to request it? The special blend implied a host of different things. She could merely be picky in regard to her taste. Or, it could mean something more.

She sipped her tea placidly while I focused on the small lavender blossoms I was attempting to stitch.

"I have just come from the Tomlinson farm," Daniel said, sweeping into the room and dropping into a chair opposite our sofa. "And I fear the problem only grows."

"The roof?" I inquired.

"No, he has begun repairs on his roof. It is his goat, Daisy. He claims Halsey, from the other side of his property line, has stolen the goat."

I could not help but be confused. Daniel had explained some of the tenant disputes in our letters. But I did not recall this one. "Can he not simply ask for his goat back?"

"But that is the rub. They are both claiming the goat is rightly theirs."

"Who is in possession of the goat now?"

Daniel rubbed a hand over his face. "Halsey." He looked tired, though his smile was ever present. Was he sleeping well in the stable rooms? "You need not concern yourself. I will sort through this."

"I should like to meet Mr. Halsey. Unless I did already?"

"You have not. He was not out when we took our tour."

I nodded. It was as I had thought. Daniel was employed for this very purpose, and I did not need to go and fix this issue. But perhaps I could. I had heard the Tomlinson name enough by now to realize the man had a penchant for arguments. Yet, he had been pleasant enough to me.

"Miss Hurst has begun a rather large project upstairs," Mrs. Overton said, breaking my musings.

"Oh?"

"She intends to repair the guest rooms."

Daniel appraised me, his eyebrows raised. "That is quite the undertaking. How do you plan to proceed?"

"One step at a time," I explained. "I should like to send out for most of the things I wish to acquire. But I am sure I can find a man in Linshire to repair a good deal of the furniture. We need not replace everything."

"You might not need to order anything either," he said, a smile growing on his lips. "Come, I've something to show you."

I remained seated, his earnest anticipation causing my breath to catch.

"It will not take long," he explained, standing. "Mrs. Overton?"

She glanced between us. "How far is it?"

He tilted his head regretfully. "Past the servants' quarters. Perhaps it is best if you do not come."

"I'm afraid the last hour has worn me out. I should rest before our dinner this evening."

Her face was pale and drawn. How horrible of me not to notice before. The woman was older, and she indeed seemed piqued. I would need to come up with a better system as our project moved forward.

I stood, clasping my hands together. "Lead the way, sir."

Daniel led me up three flights of stairs toward a small door at the far end of the corridor. "I discovered this in my initial inventory of the house."

I nodded. He stepped in first, and I followed him up the dim stairs. Light swirled above our heads, highlighting floating dust particles through the dormer windows. The slanted roof forced me to bend so as not to hit my head, and I followed Daniel to the taller side of the room.

He swept his arm forward, indicating a multitude of sheets covering lumps of various shapes and sizes.

"Daniel," I said, tamping down my smile. "You do realize I cannot see what is under the sheets, yes?"

He chuckled. He drew away a few of the sheets nearest us and I gasped. It was an entire bed frame in a gaudy, Baroque style. Beside it, he unveiled a wardrobe in matching style and a small table.

"It is enough furniture to fill a bedroom."

"Precisely," he agreed.

"Is all of this furniture?"

He nodded. "Most of it is. It is enough to get you started, at least."

"Yes. More than enough." I turned to Daniel, surprised to find him grinning at me. "It looks familiar. Where have I seen it before?"

"My bedchamber," he answered. "It had matched the rest of the floor before I made a few small changes."

"Changes for the better," I said. "You saved me from doing that one room. But how am I to get everything down?"

"You do employ a multitude of servants, Freya."

I laughed. Of course, the servants.

"Shall we begin?" he asked.

That was not part of my plan. The point of this plan was to use this project to put more space between Daniel and myself. "I am sure you have too much on your plate already. You needn't bother yourself with this."

"I enjoy it," he said softly, gazing into my eyes with a gentleness that caused my breathing to quicken. I needed to get out of the cramped attic promptly.

I stepped back. "Surely Tomlinson and Halsey will be enough of a chore for the time being."

"I have a feeling they will sort through their issues right away after receiving a word from the mistress of Corden Hall."

I had said I would speak to them, hadn't I?

I was stuck. I turned away, moving toward the stairs with purpose. I could hear Daniel replacing the sheets behind me as I descended the stairs.

This project suddenly seemed much more complicated than I had originally intended it to be.

Fairlinn Court was elegant. Long, even columns lined the front of the house with dark windows set evenly on each side of the front portico. Our carriage pulled into the drive at dusk. The light stone wall glowed orange from the remaining sun and torches lined the entry. Mr. Heybourne and his wife greeted our party, and it was clear at once we were not the only people invited. I should have assumed, with our numbers so heavy in females, that the Heybournes would need to do something to even them up.

Mrs. Overton was set upon at once by Mrs. Bennington and I wanted to stay by her side, to protect the small woman from Mrs. Bennington's vulgar claws. They moved into a corner and took seats on a couch, appearing to have a comfortable coze. I could see it for what it was, however; an inquisition.

"I am delighted you could make it," Mrs. Heybourne said beside me, threading her arm through mine as she led me toward a set of chairs before the fireplace. A large dog lounged in front of the fire, taking me off guard.

Mrs. Heybourne noticed my reaction. "Do not mind Tiny, he is harmless. He usually sleeps with Thomas, but my son has a lingering cough and keeps Tiny barking all night long. No one can get any sleep around here."

"I hope he recovers quickly," I said, concerned.

"It is nothing," she replied, waving away my unease. "He just caught a chill. He'll be right as rain in a matter of days."

Mrs. Bowen occupied a nearby seat and beamed at me. She was apparently not too upset that I had to beg off the dinner at her house when Elsie and Lord Cameron visited. Leaning forward, she said, "I cannot wait to introduce you to my sons, Miss Hurst."

A sudden wariness overtook me. Politeness forced me to say, "I would be pleased to meet them, I am sure."

She stood straightaway, her round cheeks beaming, and cupped her hand under my elbow, pulling me toward a small group of men before I even had a chance to sit. Apparently, she had taken my words as a request, and I caught Mrs. Heybourne's surprised expression as I was dragged away.

"This is Miss Hurst," Mrs. Bowen announced with all the enthusiasm of a fresh puppy. Turning to me, she proudly introduced her sons. "Alfred, John, Lucas, and the youngest one there is Henry."

I curtsied to the men. I would not have guessed that the four tall, blond, handsome men before me were the offspring of Mr. and Mrs. Bowen. The men were neither short nor portly, and while their parents possessed fair hair, that was just about the only trait they held in common.

Except, perhaps, the nose. If one squinted.

The men were as interested in me as they might be in a set of fashion plates. I received perfunctory smiles and nods before attention was arrested elsewhere.

"Miss Hurst is the owner of Corden Hall," Mrs. Bowen said. Four sets of eyes instantly snapped toward me.

"Fine, fine farmlands you have there, Miss Hurst."

"Prime hunters. I've seen them with my own eyes."

"What about the wood?" One of them said to the rest. "I've heard it's ideal for pheasants. Doesn't get hunted much, though, as it stands."

"As it *was*," another pointed out. "Now it's inhabited. I'm sure their pheasant need has doubled. What say you, Miss Hurst? Do you need any help hunting your woods?"

My eyes rounded to capacity, I was sure, and I had no inclination of what I should say. It was the precise time a companion would come in handy.

An idea formed and I grasped it. It was precisely the time that my companion *would* come in handy. "Please excuse me, gentlemen, but I must check on my friend."

They all bowed dutifully and I escaped to where Mrs. Overton was now surrounded by the matrons of the room. I was worried for her but found her smiling politely, listening to Mrs. Bennington explain Thomas's rigid schedule.

"This house is run like a tight ship. My son-in-law does not do anything by halves."

I wanted to sigh, but I swallowed the urge. Mrs. Heybourne was seated beside her mother now and listened avidly to the older women's conversation.

She moved over on the sofa to make room for me, and I sat beside her. Her smile became conspiratorial, worrying me. "I have done my duty as hostess and placed you in the most advantageous seat I could. You're welcome."

Smiling tightly, I only nodded. I had dealt with this frequently, regardless of my scandal. People constantly believed my sole purpose in life was to wed and they were doing me an immense favor by finding men to complete the job.

It was so difficult for them to imagine that I might be content with my place in life. Or, perhaps it did not occur to them at all.

Mrs. Heybourne possessed the same even-tempered cordiality as her husband, and I could not find it within myself to complain about her *efforts* or put them down. I delivered a bland smile and stood when dinner was announced.

It was to my chagrin that I found I was seated between two

of the Misters Bowen. Perhaps I should have put down Mrs. Heybourne's efforts after all to avoid a repeat in the future.

"How long have you been in residence at Corden Hall?" the one to my left asked after he had seated me. I could not remember his name for the life of me.

"Not too long," I said, pulling my gloves from my fingers and setting them on my lap. "I have been in London recently." A small voice in the back of my mind rang a warning bell but I did not know to what it was referring, this man, or the topic of conversation.

"I love London. I have been there for most of the last five years." His eyes squinted at me thoughtfully and I felt the warning bell ding again.

I promptly faced forward, waiting for a shift in the conversation partners.

"Which part of Town did you reside in?"

"Mayfair," I said, as though I had nothing to hide. Which was almost true. My eyes sought out Daniel's where he sat on the other side of the table. He faced away from me, listening intently to a woman I hadn't before met. She had pale blonde hair and was around my age, if not older than me. I felt jealousy sprinkle through me and scowled, irritated by the man beside me and the other one across the table.

"How strange," Mr. Bowen said, "that I have not met you in Town."

"I've spent the last six months in mourning." I did not continue an explanation. He did not need one. "Do you have a favorite venue in Town?"

"I do." His eyes lit up. "I am not one for stuffy ballrooms, but a fine woman can be spotted at card parties. I must say I've never been opposed to a proper dinner, either. As long as the menu is done well." He leaned in. "Mrs. Heybourne selects a decent menu for a country gathering, but it is nothing compared to the hostesses of Town."

I nodded slightly. I would not agree to slander against my host. It was rather tacky.

"You've experienced the Season in London, then?" he asked.

"Yes, quite a few." I tried not to sound too dry, but it was unseemly of him to inquire, and I felt like reminding him of my aged status. Perhaps it would put him off my scent. If he looked too closely, he might discover things about me I'd prefer to keep from this parish.

Like the status of my birth, for instance.

CHAPTER 14

The women were directed to the drawing room following dinner and the men remained behind to talk of horses and drink brandy. I felt comfortable the moment I left the Bowen brothers' sides. I could not place precisely what about them left me feeling so uneasy, but it was clear the moment we were separated that something had.

Mrs. Heybourne descended upon me like a hawk on a mouse, clutching my arm with her soft talons and pulling me to a sofa along the back wall. It occurred to me as I sat that the furniture in the room had been rearranged, the carpets rolled up and placed along the wall. While we had eaten dinner, the servants, apparently, had converted the drawing room into a dance floor.

Her eager eyes caused me to wish I had good things to say about my experience at dinner. She was so proud of her seating arrangement. "How were your dinner partners?"

"They were cordial," I said.

Mrs. Heybourne leaned forward, her eyes perfectly round. "Yes, and?"

"And they were conversational."

She slumped back on the couch slightly, looking disappointed. "They appeared eager to me."

"Yes," I agreed. "They were that."

She rallied, giving me a soft smile. "We've time yet. How are you liking Linshire?"

"It is certainly growing on me." I swallowed my frustration. Was it so hard to believe that the foremost thought in my head *wasn't* eligible gentlemen? I offered her a strained smile. She did have good intentions, I was sure. "I have lived in the center of a busy metropolis for such a long time I had forgotten the advantages of a quiet, simpler life."

She nodded in agreeance. "I have always felt that way. I did venture into Town once for a Season, but it was not exactly my cup of tea. I was glad to have met my Mr. Heybourne, for now I never have to go back."

That was the opposite of how I had felt in the beginning. I loved the Season. The balls and dances and dinners were fun. It was not until the scandal erupted that I began dreading social engagements. In fact, it had not occurred to me until this moment that I had felt little worry before attending the Heybourne's dinner party. The man who once wished to marry me was not my first choice in a neighbor, perhaps, but the family was exceedingly friendly and inclusive. I could not ask for better neighbors in that regard. Except for Mrs. Bennington, of course.

"I knew your husband, actually," I ventured, swallowing a small lump in my throat. "We were introduced by my dear friend Lady Cameron Nichols—she was Elsie Cox at the time—as they were previously acquainted from a holiday in Bath."

Her face stilled, her mouth set in a firm smile. Had I said something I shouldn't?

"My husband told me about your earlier acquaintanceship," she said. "You'll understand I can only be grateful your courtship never amounted to anything."

"I would expect no less." The tension between us pulled taut, her face a picture of discomfort. I did not regret my words, for I was grateful to know Mr. Heybourne disclosed our past with his wife. My worry stemmed from not knowing precisely how much he had shared with her.

Was my scandal to become common knowledge in this town? I had hoped I would be able to avoid it for at least a little longer.

The door opened, welcoming the men into the room, and Mrs. Heybourne stood as though her seat had caught fire beneath her. "You'll excuse me."

I nodded, but she did not see. She was gone already.

"We will have dancing," Mr. Heybourne said, his grin spreading as his wife approached him. "And music as well, if any of the ladies might be persuaded?"

The woman who sat beside Daniel during dinner stood, her hands neatly clasped before her. "I would love to play." Her voice was softer than I anticipated, meeker.

"Capital!" Mr. Heybourne called.

I was approached by a Mr. Bowen, the one who had sat to my right during dinner. We hadn't had much opportunity for conversation, his brother taking up a larger amount of my time. His expression of achievement as he led me to the center of the room was obvious. It hinted of competition, and I was not pleased to be considered in such a light.

"Do you have a favorite dance?" he asked.

I had, at one point. I loved to waltz. At present, however, I was only grateful to be dancing once again. Regardless of my obnoxious partner, I did enjoy this particular pastime. It was not with large regret or hesitation that I decided to ignore the man guiding me and simply enjoy the dance. It was not a marriage proposal, after all.

Every member of the younger set had obtained a partner and lined up for a country dance. It was lively, and I was surprised by the tune. The meek blonde woman, I had thought, would choose something more sedate. A quadrille, perhaps, or a minuet.

I peeked down the line and found Daniel partnered with the other woman I had not yet been introduced to. It was clear that she was some relation to the woman playing the piano and my curiosity rose. A younger sister, perhaps? He had an easy way about him in their presence; it begged an explanation.

I supposed I ought to focus on my own partner and simply be grateful Miss Chappelle had not been invited to the Heybournes' dinner party that evening. Not the most charitable thought, perhaps. But I did appreciate her absence, nonetheless.

"Well?"

I glanced sharply at my partner. He had asked me a question earlier, had he not? I could not recall what it was. To my relief, the dance began. I found myself smiling, enjoying myself. It mattered not that my partner was a total stranger with zero interest in me before my estate was announced. I tried not to mind that two of the women I met in this new town had already begun matchmaking schemes at my very first social event.

They had good intentions, I supposed. There was no use feeling offended. Instead, I lost myself in the rapid motions and quick-footed steps of the country dance. By the end of the song I was grinning at no one in particular, my chest heaving from the exertion and sweat beading around the edges of my hairline and back of my neck.

It was exceedingly warm in the room, the heat only growing from the dancing.

"We shall have a quadrille!" Mr. Heybourne announced.

My eyes landed on Daniel, and I was startled to find him staring at me. Would he ask me to dance? My body hummed with anticipation as he took a step forward. The mere thought of placing my gloved hand within his was enough to set my heart to a gallop—a remarkable feat when it was already beating hard from the previous dance.

A second Mr. Bowen stepped into my line of sight and bowed. "May I have the honor of this dance, Miss Hurst?"

I could no longer see Daniel. He was blocked from my view by this giant blond man. Regret pooled in my shoulders, dragging them downward, but I maintained a polite smile, nodding and placing my hand in his.

I had not sat by this particular Mr. Bowen at dinner. He was the youngest of the lot; that much I did recall. We took our places in preparation. The older set was sitting out this round and I caught Mrs. Overton's eye before the music began. She had faint lines between her eyebrows, confusion drawn on her face.

It was not the moment to inquire, but I would have liked to ease her worry, whatever it was. I planned then to go and sit with her when the quadrille ended.

The youngest Mr. Bowen was graceful, leading me through the steps with a polish I had not noticed in his older brother. He did not try to hold a conversation, for which I was much obliged, and I was equally gratified to find Daniel partnering Mrs. Heybourne.

Not that it mattered whom he danced with, of course. But the more matrons, the better, in my opinion.

Mr. Bowen bowed over my hand on completion of the dance and I turned for Mrs. Overton, disappointed to find Mrs. Bennington seated beside her. The older woman had not left her side for much of the evening. The fact, while seemingly harmless, left me uneasy.

"You seem to enjoy the dancing," Mrs. Overton said as I sat beside her.

One of the older Misters Bowen was attempting to convince the blonde woman at the pianoforte to take a turn on the dance floor and allow another young woman the opportunity to play. I watched his efforts with some amusement.

"I have always enjoyed dancing," I replied. "Mourning has required that I sit out for the last six months, and I find that I've missed it exceedingly." Not that I'd had many dance partners before that, either, in recent years.

Mrs. Overton nodded knowingly. Mrs. Bennington turned an eagle eye on me. "Mourning," she said. "How sad."

I was not going to bite the bait. "It is a necessary season in most lives. This was mine."

I could not ask Mrs. Overton what had bothered her earlier with Mrs. Bennington nearby. The predatory woman was on the hunt. If I stayed nearby then she would surely sniff out my scandal. It was only a matter of time. I stood. "If you'll excuse me."

Mr. Bowen was still in the act of convincing the blonde woman to leave the pianoforte. I approached them, my hands clasped before me. The party had broken off into small groups of conversation, no one seeming to notice or mind that the music had stopped.

"I should like to play," I said to the woman. "If you would like to dance."

She eyed me, her face looking tired in a way I had not noticed at a distance. She looked to Mr. Bowen and said, "Pray introduce us, sir?"

He was surprised, but recovered quickly. "Mrs. Wheeler, allow me to present Miss Hurst."

"Of Corden Hall?" Mrs. Wheeler asked, her face betraying her lack of surprise. She already knew who I was. I fought the urge to glance at Daniel where he spoke to the Heybournes a few yards away. Had he spoken about me at dinner?

I nodded. "Yes. Do you live nearby?"

"In town," she answered. "My sister and I keep house for our brother."

The other blonde woman must've been her sister, then.

She smiled at me then, and I liked her despite my reservations. Her title implied marriage, but there was no mention of a husband. Off at sea, perhaps?

"Allow me to play?" I asked. She stepped aside and Mr. Bowen beamed.

"A waltz, Miss Hurst?" he asked.

I nodded, seating myself on the bench. Mr. Bowen took Mrs. Wheeler's hand and led her to the center of the room. I warmed up my fingers on the keys, aware through my peripheral vision of men slowly asking women to dance.

Mrs. Overton remained seated, Mrs. Bennington beside her. The remaining guests were dancing, aside from two of the Bowen men, seated in the corner, and Daniel.

I nearly lost my place as he approached the pianoforte, but continued play. The transition was smooth enough that I hoped the dancers had not noticed.

"Would you like me to turn the pages?" he asked.

I looked to the empty place where music would normally be placed and gave Daniel a small smile before glancing back at my hands. I was playing from memory, but I could not glance away for long or the distraction would cause me to falter again.

"I thank you, sir, but it is unnecessary."

He chuckled. "I see that now."

"You do not wish to dance?" I asked, watching my fingers glide along the ivory keys. I had always enjoyed playing the pianoforte, and though I could not claim any particular talent for it, I was tolerable enough.

"I did not say that."

I glanced at him quickly before watching my fingers again, my cheeks warming at the look in his eyes. Swallowing, I ventured for a light tone. "Mrs. Overton does not wish to dance?"

"She would prefer to rest her feet."

I could not keep the smile from my lips. "And Mrs. Bennington?"

While I did not look at Daniel, he sounded as though a smile sat on his lips as well. "She would prefer to keep Mrs. Overton company. It is kind of her."

"Perhaps."

I hazarded a glance at the dancers, pleased to see Mrs. Bowen dancing with her husband, and Mrs. Heybourne with hers. Mrs. Wheeler was partnered with the older Mr. Bowen, and the blonde woman who I assumed to be her sister was dancing with another of the Misters Bowen.

Perhaps it would benefit me to learn their names, but for now I was satisfied without that knowledge.

Daniel's voice lowered slightly. "Have you enjoyed yourself this evening?"

"It has been satisfactory. Dinner was delicious."

"Yes, I agree. And your table partners?"

"Talkative."

He laughed, and warmth washed over me. It was a deep, smooth sound and I enjoyed hearing it very much.

"One of the Misters Bowen would like to come and hunt in the wood," I said. "He believes we could use some help stocking the kitchen. And another one mentioned your prime hunters. At least, I am assuming he was speaking about your hunters. Do I own any hunters?"

"No, you do not," he answered with amusement. "Which of them was it? I would like to know if he has an eye to buy."

"I could not tell you his name," I said honestly. "Though he sat beside me at dinner. The one to my left." The inquisitive one, I almost added.

"Ah, Mr. John Bowen. I shall have to speak to him."

"Gathering buyers?"

"Not entirely. But I would never refuse the opportunity to discuss horses."

I smiled, though I did not understand the feeling. I enjoyed riding, of course, but I was not horse mad as so many men were.

I brought the song to a close and rolled my shoulders, pushing out my arms and stretching my fingers. Light clapping reached my ears and I turned to smile, only to be struck by Daniel's intent gaze fixed on my own. I was aware of my mouth hanging open, and I promptly closed it, turning back to the pianoforte when another waltz was requested by Mr. Heybourne.

I noticed Daniel walk away but I did not watch to see who he approached. I played a few measures more before hazarding a glance and swallowed my disappointment to find his arms wrapped around Mrs. Wheeler. She was lovely, if my short meeting was any indication. I had liked her once she'd turned her own smile on me. I believed I was a sound judge of character, and the one I saw in her countenance was good which made the smile on Daniel's face squeeze my gut all the more.

I could not fault him for enjoying a waltz with a kind woman. But I *could* do my best to discover her matrimonial situation.

Not that it mattered, for I was secure in my dusty place on the shelf, and I was certainly not having romantic feelings toward my steward. That would be pure folly.

I passed the remainder of the dance with my eyes fixed securely on my fluid fingers. It was a song I played often and knew well. Simpler, perhaps, than these fine people were used to. But it kept the count just the same.

When the song came to completion, I stood to more polite clapping. Curtseying, I crossed the room to sit beside Mrs. Overton.

"Your playing is lovely," she said.

"That is kind. I am aware my talent is not above average. Still, I enjoy it."

"Isn't that the objective of most things?" she asked softly. "To enjoy them?"

Mrs. Bennington tittered. "If that were my guiding rule, I find I would be quite larger than I am at present. It does not do to place the focus of our lives on enjoyment unless we want to become slothful and let idleness lead our lives."

Clearly Mrs. Bennington had great restraint. I found I did not need to fear idleness so greatly.

"Unless," I countered, "we find that joy through worthwhile pursuits."

"No one would continue to find pure enjoyment in serving others if that were all one did with their time."

"It is healthy to have a balance, naturally," I agreed, "but I believe we are allowed a certain level of merely joyful pursuits outside of service."

I had lost her there. Or she was simply uninterested. Mrs. Overton, on the other hand, seemed intrigued. "And how would you spend your time if you were not worried over the things you needed to do and simply created a schedule based off what you wished to do?"

"I would not concern myself with the things that brought me anxiety," I answered quickly. "I would like to learn the finer art of gardening, and I love to read, play the pianoforte, and knit."

Mrs. Bennington scoffed. "Fine pursuits, indeed."

I tried to push away the defensiveness that naturally rose within me.

But Mrs. Overton spoke on my behalf, bringing herself to a stand. "I think they are lovely pursuits. If it would please you, Miss Hurst, I believe I had better be getting home."

"Of course." I stood as well, before turning. "Good evening, Mrs. Bennington. A pleasure."

I located my hosts and led Mrs. Overton to them straight away.

"Thank you for a lovely evening," I said, careful to direct my smile to Mrs. Heybourne.

"You are quite welcome. We enjoyed your company."

"Do not be a stranger," Mr. Heybourne said, the jovial smile I knew well plastered on his face. "We are always around if you find yourself in need. Though I know you've got a wonderful steward in Mr. Bryce."

"And the superb company of Mrs. Overton," Mrs. Heybourne added, including my companion.

Daniel approached us. He had read our intentions, apparently, for he was prepared to lead us out to the carriage. He thanked our hosts and confirmed a meeting with Mr. Heybourne to look at horses.

The earlier conversation I held with Mrs. Heybourne played over in my mind as I observed her watching her husband. She had seemed artless on our first meeting. Now I did not know what to think. This woman, perhaps, knew my biggest secret.

I needed to discern if she was an ally or an enemy. And quickly.

CHAPTER 15

Daniel swept from the study door and down the corridor with such haste that I jumped back to avoid a collision.

"Do forgive me," he said, stepping back.

"What is it?" I asked, my hand on my heart to calm it.

He shook his head. "The goat."

I awaited more information but none was forthcoming. "Come again, sir?"

Running a hand over his face, he shifted on his feet. Irritation was written upon his features. "I just received word Tomlinson and Halsey are fighting over that blasted goat again." His eyes caught mine sharply. "Forgive me. That was out of line."

"Are you going now to address it?"

He nodded.

"Take me with you?"

"I could not. I told you that you could let me handle this. It is my job."

"And I recall you mentioning that Tomlinson finds me intimidating. Perhaps I could intimidate them into sharing properly."

A lopsided smile found its way onto his lips and his dimple appeared. I trained my gaze on his eyes instead so as not to be caught staring. "Very well," he said, offering me his arm. "It is worth trying."

Daniel requested two horses and we pulled ourselves up into their saddles before I followed him toward the tenant farms. The roof of the Tomlinson cottage was looking far better than the last time I'd seen it and a woman sat in the yard scrubbing cloth in a sudsy bucket.

"Good day, Mrs. Tomlinson," Daniel called. "Where might I find your husband?"

"Where do you think?" she countered, eyeing me with apprehension. "Arguing over that dratted goat again."

Daniel tipped his hat to the woman before leading his horse around the house. I smiled at her before following him, and her wary eyes watched me until we were out of sight.

"Should I buy them another goat? Do tell me they are not struggling so hard that a goat might make the difference."

"She's a pet," Daniel answered wryly.

I could not help but giggle. All this over a pet goat? I considered Coco and my cats. If someone tried to steal them from me, I would be upset, too. I supposed it made sense. I watched Daniel comfortably trot along.

"I won't leave! Try and force me. I'll be here all day and all night." The gruff voice sounded like he meant it.

We rounded a corner and came upon two men standing on either side of a livestock pen. A content gray goat stood in the center, lazily chewing on grass.

"You've got nothing on me," the other man said.

"Gentlemen," Daniel called, forcing the two farmers to quit glaring across the pen and turn to face us. I slid from my horse, shocking Tomlinson and Halsey, and handed the horse's reins to Daniel.

"Good day," I said. "I am Miss Hurst. What a lovely goat you have here, gentlemen."

Tomlinson was the first to recover. He bowed. "Miss Hurst, she is lovely indeed. My little Daisy is a prize."

"She'll catch me a prize when the fair comes back through. She does tricks," Halsey explained, puffing out his ample belly.

Clearly the goat belonged to Tomlinson. If I needed any proof, it was the look of disgust on his rugged features over Halsey's comment.

A thud behind me called my attention, and I turned to watch Daniel tie our horses' leads to a tree.

"What if we compromise?" I asked. Both men gave me their attention. I felt ridiculous discussing the ownership of a pet goat, but it had to be done. "The fair is not here now, is it?"

Both men shook their heads.

"Then we shall strike a deal. When the time comes to utilize Daisy for her tricks and earn a prize, Mr. Halsey may take her to the fair and try his hand at it. On the condition"—I raised my arm to stem Mr. Tomlinson's argument—"that you split the proceeds in half, and Mr. Tomlinson takes care of her in the interim."

Blank faces stared back at me.

"Mr. Tomlinson takes Daisy home *now* and cares for her until the fair," I explained. It was an unfair trade when Halsey had stolen the poor man's goat, but this way they would both get what they were after.

"Ouch."

I turned to find Daniel coming toward me, his eyebrows pulled together as he inspected the palm of his hand. "I'm not sure how this happened," he said, showing me his palm.

My stomach began to swirl. Vivid red mixed with pale skin before me, causing bile to climb up my throat. I felt pinpricks in the outer corners of my eyes and stepped forward, grabbing the edge of the pen to hold myself upright.

"Freya, what is it?" Daniel asked, concerned.

"Your hand."

"'Tis nothing. Only a scratch."

I swallowed, watching Daisy happily chew on another bite of grass. Or perhaps it was the same one she'd been chewing before.

"No," I clarified. "The blood."

My words brought the image of his hand to my mind again, and I quickly discovered that the pen was not sufficient to hold me upright. I managed to say, "I am not fond of blood," before my eyes closed in and darkness swept me to the ground.

Something was poking me in the small of my back. Many tiny, sharp needles made their way through my clothing and pricked my skin. My eyelids, heavy and thick, struggled to open against the bright sunlight.

"She's coming to," a gruff voice said.

"You might step back then," another snapped.

"The both of you could cease your arguing altogether," said a third. This one, I recognized. "Miss Hurst?" he asked. I forced my eyes open and was gratified by the green eyes trained on me.

His smile was apologetic, his eyes downturned in regret. When my eyes opened all the way, I made to sit up.

"Wait," Daniel said. "You must not rise too quickly."

"I cannot stay down here," I countered. "The grass is itchy."

He covered his surprise quickly and helped me sit. "You never told me of your weakness for…"

I glanced to his hand but it was wrapped in linen. I turned my head away when the swirling in my stomach began.

"Have you sorted the mess with Daisy?"

He smiled at me. "No. But you did. The men are agreeable."

I could hear their faint arguing from where they waited a few yards away. Agreeable might be something of a stretch, but I understood his meaning. "They've agreed to let Mr. Tomlinson care for her?"

Daniel nodded. "Brilliant, really. Halsey doesn't care about the thing. This way Tomlinson gets his goat back and part of the winnings if, indeed, Halsey wins a prize." He watched me closely. "Do you think you can ride back?"

"Yes." I used his arm to pull myself to a stand and landed far closer to him than I intended. My hand rested on his forearm, snug between us, and I caught his intense gaze, his nostrils flaring as though he struggled to breathe through his nose. Earthy tones mixed with shaving soap, and I wanted to lean in further to fill my senses with his scent. His eyes fell to my lips and rested there momentarily.

I stepped back, releasing his arm and clutching my skirts. "Let us go home."

"There is a rumor circling about you," Daniel said, effectively halting me in my tracks in the center of the drawing room carpet. The tea, however, did not pause as efficiently as I did, and sloshed from the cup I held, splattering over the front of my gown and down on the carpet.

"Good heavens!" he said, jumping from his chair with a napkin in tow. He thrust it at me, and I set my teacup on the small side table and mopped up the liquid from my gown as best I could.

"I apologize, heartily."

"Do not fret." I tried to sound calm, but a storm of emotions raged within me, none of them relating to tea. I'd had no inclination I was being spoken of to begin with, but a rumor? There was no such thing as a positive rumor. The nature of the thing itself was speaking about others without their knowledge.

It had been a week since the dinner party at Fairlinn Park, and Daniel had not seen anyone since that night, to my knowledge. Had he been keeping this a secret from me for that long?

"Please be seated." He guided me to the sofa before moving across the room to prepare a fresh cup of tea.

Mrs. Overton had gone for an afternoon nap, her delicate nature still adjusting to the pace at Corden Hall. While there was no particular industry to the house or our way of living, it was significantly larger than her last one, according to Daniel, and she had yet to grow used to the many stairs and expansive rooms.

She would get there eventually, I believed. But the restorative nature of an afternoon rest had become essential in allowing Mrs. Overton to continue later into the evenings.

Because of this, she had excused herself from my restoration project, leaving Daniel and me to fix up the bedrooms with the help of the servants. We had nearly completed the first room and were preparing to move onto the next.

Daniel brought me a fresh cup of tea and I set it on the table, allowing it time to cool. "The rumor?" I inquired. My voice wavered, and I hoped he had not caught that detail.

He shook his head dismissively, sitting on the other end of the sofa. "It is nothing, really."

I waited, hoping to appear patient when in reality I was slowly tensing up. Could he sense that? He watched me closely. Though that could have been because of the sudden scare he'd caused. I wanted to forget all sense of decorum and beg him to put me from my misery—or bring me closer to the eventuality I tried to prepare myself for.

My white knuckles gripped the edge of the seat cushion and my breathing became shallow. Clearly I had not fully prepared myself for my past to become public knowledge. What was taking him so long?

"Yes?" I said, unable to wait any longer.

"I met with Mr. Heybourne this morning."

I would have fainted, I think, if not for the sudden knock at the door. My head whipped around to find Harrison standing in the open doorway.

"The post has come, ma'am."

He brought me a few letters, one sealed with a familiar crest, and I found myself growing even more desperate despite rational thought. I appreciated Rosalynn's updates, but she would have to wait for now. I set the missive on my lap and looked at Daniel expectantly, brushing a lock of hair from my face.

"Would you like some privacy to read your letters?"

Of all the ridiculous things. Of course I did not want privacy. I wanted—no, *needed* to know exactly what rumor had finally made its way to the small community of Linshire. "They can wait a moment."

"Heybourne heard from his wife that you are to throw a ball. Apparently, it is the talk of the town."

That was all? I felt air fill my lungs as my shoulders relaxed subtly. "I would be happy to throw a ball."

He raised an eyebrow in question. Or perhaps it was mere disbelief.

"I love to dance," I defended. And I would throw a hundred balls if it meant people talked about them instead of my father's indiscretions. I picked up my tea and took a sip, the warm liquid improving my mood at once.

"I noticed."

I glanced up sharply. Had he been watching me the night of the Heybournes' dinner party? There was no other explanation.

"And," he continued, as if he hadn't said anything of worthwhile consideration, "if you throw a ball yourself, you could hire musicians and dance every single dance."

I laughed, unable to hold in the vision that created. "It has been years since I've danced every dance, sir. I do not anticipate any such success. Nor do I wish it."

"You said yourself you love to dance."

"I also enjoy full feeling in my toes. I am no longer up to the standard of dancing into the wee hours of the night."

He shook his head. "You speak of yourself as though you are ancient."

"Compared to the debutantes—"

"There are no debutantes here." The force of his tone knocked the rest of my thought away. His serious eyes locked on me with a severity that frightened me. I was not afraid of Daniel, but of the feelings he caused within me.

I stood, clasping my letters like a lifeline. "I must go and change my gown."

The heat of his gaze seared me while I walked from the room, propelling me forward and away from him. I did not like the uncertain warmth flowing through me. I did not appreciate the way Daniel was causing me to question myself, my feelings, or my basic values.

He was throwing a rock into my perfectly orchestrated plan for my life, and I needed another outlet.

I needed to focus on something else—*anything* else. A ball was the perfect thing.

I bathed and changed my dress, giving the soiled gown to Tilly to clean, and found Mrs. Overton in the morning room. We shared a love for the room. Though it was not primely lit in the afternoon, the smaller size and comfortable sofas were enough to draw both of us to it in preference to the large drawing room most days.

I was grateful for Mrs. Overton. She was easy to be around, and I appreciated her ability to balance between acting my chaperone and giving me my needed privacy. I received a letter from my mother along with Rosalynn's update, and she refused my invitation to come yet again. This time, however, she cited the *rundown house* as cause for discomfort. I could only assume she had experienced the Corden Hall of the past. I was determined to write her a detailed outline of the changes Daniel and I were making and convince her to see that the house was comfortable.

I sat on the sofa, pulling my embroidery out to finish the lilac tree.

"I heard about the spill," Mrs. Overton said diplomatically.

"It was a bit of a mess, but I feel better now." I sat beside her on the sofa. I had pulled Coco from the master's suite, where she spent the majority of her time, and brought her downstairs with me. "Would you like to accompany me into Linshire tomorrow? I saw a shop with yarn during my last visit and I would like to obtain a variety. I also need to choose some fabric for the drapes in the bedchambers we are doing over. They are both nearly ready."

"That would be lovely. I am in need of some new stockings. Daniel has been kind enough to keep me stocked in the things that I need, but I find I cannot request such an item from him."

I shared a knowing smile with the older woman. "No man would wish to run such an errand. It is settled. We will go to town in the morning."

CHAPTER 16

Daniel had the grace to avoid the topic of my tea spill at dinner that evening, and he was nothing but bland, distant courtesy at breakfast the following morning. Had he sensed my fear of his attentions and decided to give me room to breathe?

I noticed the bandage missing from his hand and refrained from asking after his injury, for I could only assume it was healed now that nothing protected his palm.

Mrs. Overton and I left for Linshire shortly after breakfast. We found the stockings she needed, as well as a bonnet I did not. It was a lovely straw confection with a sprig of white silk flowers and a lovely green ribbon. It was such a delightful contrast to my bright hair that I could not help but purchase it.

Despite the shopkeeper's avid sales tactics, I was not under the impression that it made my face glow or my eyes sparkle. I did think it was lovely, and that was sufficient for me.

I filled a large basket with a plethora of yarn. Enough to cause my companion's eyebrows to raise in inquiry. I simply smiled at her and tucked the basket handle over my arm.

"Would you like to look at the bookshop?"

She agreed and we let ourselves into a small shop that smelled of candles. A dangerous scent, perhaps, for a building full of books.

Walking the aisles as Mrs. Overton slowly perused the section of gothic novels, I tried not to look too shocked when she selected one and purchased it.

I caught sight of a familiar leather-bound book in the corner of the front window as we left and paused in spite of myself. *The Green Door.* It was years ago the book had swept through Society, filling London's drawing rooms with gossip and intrigue and setting the stage for the rumor that would, effectively, change my entire life.

"Are you well, dear?" Mrs. Overton asked, her small, wrinkled face full of concern.

Nodding, I turned toward the carriage. I was tempted to go back inside and buy the book simply to remove it from the shopkeeper's window. But I found I could not bring myself to do it.

I did not notice Miss Chappelle until she stepped directly in front of me. "*Bonjour*, Miss Hurst."

I curtseyed, tucking an errant curl behind my ear. "Miss Chappelle, allow me to introduce my friend, Mrs. Overton."

Pleasantries were exchanged, and Mrs. Overton looked between the dark beauty and myself, her face an unreadable mask.

"How are you adjusting to small country life?" Miss Chappelle asked.

"It is not much of an adjustment," I said. "I spent nearly my whole life in the country before moving to London."

"And your parents?" she asked, her eyes dark and intelligent, never leaving my face. "Where are they now?"

I felt the blood drain from my face. I had the distinct feeling she knew precisely where my parents were, and it terrified me. I swallowed, my eyes flicking back to the book in the shop window of their own accord.

Mrs. Overton spoke, her voice firm. "I do apologize, Miss Chappelle, but we must be getting on."

"Yes, of course." She nodded, stepping out of our way. Her dark eyes watched me with a calmness that was far from reassuring.

Mrs. Overton gripped my arm with a strength I did not realize she possessed and directed me toward the carriage. We gave the footman our packages and my basket full of yarn and climbed into the vehicle.

"I am quite careful when speaking ill of others, but I cannot refrain at present, and I hope you will forgive me," Mrs. Overton said, her voice calm and clear. "But I do not like that woman."

I looked out the window as the carriage rolled forward, all of the secrets in my past piling up and weighing me down. I did not like her either.

We sat in the drawing room that evening, and I pulled the basket out from under the sofa where I had stashed it earlier.

"What are you creating?" Daniel asked, seating himself beside Mrs. Overton and across from me.

"A baby blanket," I answered. "A friend of mine is about to add another little one to her household."

"That is very kind of you."

"Yes, well, I happen to know firsthand that she cannot knit. And the poor child will have to endure a trip across the country at a very tender age. I am merely being practical."

"Practicality aside," Mrs. Overton said, "it *is* kind of you."

I looked at my lap, focusing on the stitches lining up on the knitting needle like small, obedient soldiers. I did not take well to praise, though I appreciated the thought. It occurred to me in that moment I had yet to read the recent letter from Rosalynn. I'd skimmed my mother's and put myself to the task of responding to her but had forgotten about the other mail.

I weighed my options in my mind and decided to wait until I went up to bed to read it. I could spend another quarter of an hour working on the blanket and then bid my housemates good night.

I turned to Mrs. Overton. "How are you adjusting to Corden Hall?"

She watched me as though measuring her words. "I had not considered becoming a companion until Daniel concocted the scheme."

I looked at him. He was watching Mrs. Overton carefully, as if her answer mattered to him a great deal.

"And while I was hesitant at first," she continued, "the experience has been considerably better than I anticipated."

"I am glad to hear that," Daniel said, his face relaxed and satisfied.

Drat proper social conventions. I wanted so badly to inquire on the nature of their relationship. I opened my mouth to ask that very question when Daniel turned to me. The light in his soft green eyes was shining. I closed my mouth. I did not want to be the cause of dimming it.

"I forgot to mention it earlier," he said, "but it seems that Coco has discovered how to get herself to the living quarters above the stables."

My hands paused and dropped in my lap. "I checked on her this morning, and she was snug in her bed in the master's chamber."

He grinned. "I brought her back inside when I came in for breakfast. She must have returned to her own room."

I shook my head, focusing on my knitting.

Mrs. Overton chuckled. "You always did have a way with the

animals. 'Tis no wonder, I suppose, you've chosen a career in horses."

Silence fell upon us. Mrs. Overton opened the book she had been holding and Daniel sat quietly.

I felt his gaze resting on me, but I could not tear my eyes away from the even, smooth motion of creating stitches.

Warmth spread across the back of my neck and moved down my body as I felt Daniel's watchful eye. I wanted to look up and see if it was a creation of my own mind or if he was, in fact, looking at me as closely as I felt he was. My fingers fumbled with the yarn and I tugged at the ball once, hoping to create more slack. The soft yellow wool rolled from the basket and away from my leg, hitting Daniel's boot in one smooth motion, as if I had intended to get his attention.

I looked up and froze. Clear, soft green eyes trained on me in a look so serene and contented that I found my own anxiety drain away.

He leaned down and picked up the yarn ball before crossing the rug and placing it in my hand. "The cats might come after that if they catch it rolling away."

I chuckled, the laugh sounding strained to my own ears.

"Thank you." I took the yarn and rolled it up again before shoving my project into the basket and under the sofa. "I think I will retire for the evening. I received a letter from a dear friend and have not yet had the opportunity to read it."

"Goodnight," Mrs. Overton said, smiling swiftly before returning to her book.

"Goodnight, Miss Hurst," Daniel said.

I curtseyed to them before making my escape, my breath coming in rapid spurts. I ran up the stairs and into my room, leaning against the door until my heart slowed considerably. Taking a seat at the writing desk beside the window, I lit a candle before sliding a penknife under Rosalynn's wax seal and unfolding the thick paper. A newspaper clipping fell onto the floor and I placed it on the desk before reading the letter.

My eyes swept through her words with haste. After the first ominous sentence, I found myself devouring the rest. It could not be true. It absolutely had to be false. Rumors often were based on lies, were they not? Elsie's experience with the newspapers in her first Season was proof enough of that.

I glanced at the clipping but returned to the letter, forcing myself to read it again slowly so that I might not miss any pertinent information.

Reading it a second time did not change the meaning. I leaned back in my chair, eyeing the newspaper clipping with disgust. I stood quickly, my chair falling back and hitting the floor with a loud thud before I righted it.

Pacing the length of the room, I came close to picking up the clipping a few more times before I sank onto the edge of my bed and dropped my head in my hands.

Hadn't the objective of coming to Corden Hall been to escape my father and his family and all connection to them? Was I not going to receive a break from the Fashionable World's scorn and gossip?

Oh, dear. Many people residing in the country received London's newspapers. How many more days would it be until the people of Linshire had read these words and made the connection?

There was nothing for it. I simply had to read the article so I knew what I was dealing with. I stood abruptly, full of determination, when a knock sounded on the door and I yelped, the timing causing me to startle.

"Freya?" a familiar voice called.

I relaxed, crossing to the door and opening it a fraction.

Pale green eyes under thick, brown brows regarded me closely. "I heard a loud sound from downstairs. I wanted to check on you and make sure everything was all right."

My cheeks warmed, and I smiled self-consciously. "I am fine. I only stood up too quickly and knocked a chair over."

"And all the pacing?"

The blush deepened. I could feel it. "You could hear that?"

His smile was easy to see, regardless of the dim lighting. I leaned against the wall with one shoulder, making sure my face was the only thing visible through the door. It was not proper for Daniel to be upstairs speaking to me alone like this, particularly outside my bedroom door. We were asking for a scandal if we were to be found.

Speaking of being found, where was Mrs. Overton?

Soft fur paws brushed over my toes, and I jumped slightly, moving back for Coco to walk through the door and circle Daniel's feet.

He bent down and picked her up, stroking her behind her ears while he trained his gaze back on me. "As long as you are not in any trouble."

"Well, I wouldn't say that." I clamped my mouth shut. The words had escaped on their own accord, and they had not missed his notice.

"What is it?"

"Just news from home. Some things I wanted to avoid are beginning to catch up with me." The weight of the realization spoken aloud was heavy on my shoulders and I felt them slump. Living through the scandal the first time had been difficult enough. If it made its way to Linshire and exploded here as well, I would have to live through the ordeal all over again. That was not something I believed myself capable of.

"Freya," he said softly, stepping closer. "What is going on?"

I wanted to tell him so badly, yet I feared his reaction. The moments of late where he had paid me special attention were seared onto my heart. I was beginning to care for this man, and, regardless of what happened in the future, I wanted to count him as one of my friends. He was undoubtedly among the most trustworthy, kind people I had met.

I had taken too long in considering whether to tell him or not because his eyebrows pulled together, concern etched on his face. "What is it?"

"I'm not entirely sure," I said honestly. "My friend sent me a note to inform me that there is an engagement, possibly, in the near future."

His eyebrows rose. I swallowed and continued. "It is a person I am related to, in a way. She sent me the newspaper clipping about it, but I cannot bring myself to read it."

"Freya, what about this is so distressing?" He stepped back suddenly, his brow lifting. "Oh, I see."

"You do?" My heart sped up. Did he already know about my illegitimacy?

"It must be very difficult for you, if you cannot bring yourself to read about it." He looked away and then back at me. "Have you cared about this person for quite some time?"

"No," I said at once. "I've never cared."

He must have been able to tell I was lying, for he gave me a slight smile before passing Coco through the doorway. I took her and she whimpered.

"I will let you go," he said. "But if I can leave a word of advice, read the article. You will be able to move on more quickly if you allow yourself to face it."

I nodded, shutting the door after a whispered farewell.

I had not expected such understanding, but then again, he probably did not fully comprehend what I was dealing with. I let Coco down and watched her walk through the adjoining door and into her room before I forced myself back to the writing table and newspaper article.

Holding the fragile paper securely in both hands, I moved closer to the candle and read the words carefully, taking in each description and insinuation and trying to make perfect sense of what was going on. It helped that Rosalynn had laid out the basic meaning of the cryptic article in her letter, and had identified the man who was likely going to propose before the end of the Season—to my half-sister.

My stomach rolled at the thought. At least I knew her name now. Adele must be the wife, because Rosalynn had called the daughter Sophie in her letter. And Sophie was making a very successful connection with a future earl. According to the article —with help from my translator, Rosalynn—Lord Melbourne was going to expire any day now and his heir was set to inherit, and marry Sophie Hurst, all in the next short while.

The first half of the article was fine. It was the second half that described the bride's estranged, illegitimate half-sister who had escaped to the country to hide in disgrace. It spoke of me as though I had run away from Sophie's beauty and intellect and clear superiority.

I dropped my hands in my lap. The whole of London was reading—and likely believing—these words. Soon, so would the rest of the country. I had escaped London to decide for myself how I felt. I did not run *away* from my father and his family. I was running toward something better.

I slumped onto the chair beside the writing desk and read over Rosalynn's letter again. She had claimed it was not as bad as it sounded, and she and Lord McGregor were doing what they could to dispel the negativity surrounding my name. And then, the clincher, she offered to fetch me from Corden Hall at once so I might face the throngs and prove to them I had nothing to hide.

Well, she was correct on one account; I did have nothing to hide. London's high Society already knew everything there was to know about me. I was a spinster, and I did avoid marriage. I did run to the country to get away from Father, Sophie and Adele. But not for the reasons they all assumed.

Anger replaced sorrow, and I picked up both sheets of paper

before shoving them into a drawer. It was not an issue, yet. Until the papers got to Linshire, I needn't do anything about it.

Even then, there was a small chance no one would make the connection that I was related to Sophie Hurst. The article did not ever actually mention her by name—it merely alluded to her.

I rang the bell to call for Tilly so I could dress for bed. I was suddenly exhausted.

CHAPTER 17

Harrison searched me out in the back garden to inform me that I had callers. I had spent the duration of the morning walking the rows of roses and hedges, unable to sit still for longer than a moment, and recommitting to replacing the dancing couple statue in the garden. The night before was filled with sporadic, fitful sleep. I had to come up with a plan regarding how I might handle any rumors that reached me in Linshire. Clearly, given my panic when Daniel mentioned the rumor of the ball, I was not prepared to handle any large scandals.

I followed Harrison inside and was slightly relieved to find Mrs. Heybourne seated on the sofa beside her mother. Mrs. Overton occupied a wingback chair opposite them, and I seated myself in the chair beside hers.

Mrs. Heybourne smiled at me as I sat, her face devoid of any sourness. I was glad she had not seemed to hold a grudge over my previous relationship with her husband. Particularly as one sided as it had been.

"I was just mentioning to my mother and Mrs. Overton," she said, "that I had such a splendid time dancing after our dinner party. I was very gratified so many of our guests were willing to do so."

"I believe dancing is widely accepted as one of the primest forms of entertainment." I laughed. "You'd be hard pressed to find a group of young people who are opposed to spending their evening dancing."

"Young people, yes," Mrs. Bennington said. "And those who are not so young anymore."

My cheeks grew warm, and I swallowed. Was she referring to me? I knew I was not fresh from the schoolroom anymore, but I'd like to think I was still agile enough to dance with enthusiasm.

"I love to dance," Mrs. Overton said. "I cannot complete those fast-paced steps the younger set is doing these days, but I could perform a Scottish reel with the best of them just a few years ago."

Mrs. Bennington nodded, all condescension. "I am sure."

"Miss Hurst," Mrs. Heybourne cut in, her wide eyes betraying enthusiasm. "Is it true you plan to hold a ball?"

Mrs. Bennington's face pinched uncomfortably. I trained my smile on her daughter. I was so unaccountably grateful they did not bring a newspaper with them to parade my shame that I would gladly throw a hundred balls.

"I am still vastly unfamiliar with the customs of Linshire and most of the people about. I could use help from a local society woman in creating a guest list."

Mrs. Heybourne looked near to bursting. "I should love to help you. When may we begin?"

I glanced to Mrs. Overton, a small smile on her lips. She nodded once and I said, "Now?"

Mrs. Heybourne agreed and we moved to the table at the other side of the room to begin planning. I had chosen the correct person from whom to ask for assistance. As soon as I gave her free rein she immediately flew away with her ideas. I would not have to do much in preparation if Mrs. Heybourne had her way, for she had a very clear idea of how a ball should be conducted at Corden Hall.

As our conversation lengthened, I found myself growing excited over the prospect of the ball as well. Mrs. Bennington fetched her daughter before we completed our plans entirely and we made a date to get together the following afternoon to complete the lists for decor and menu items and create a guest list.

Once the women left, I sat beside Mrs. Overton again.

"I appreciate your assistance." I stretched my arms and glanced at the woman. "I do not believe we would have achieved half as much without the uninterrupted time."

"It was the least I could do. Mrs. Bennington likes to speak; I merely needed to listen."

I had the sense that Mrs. Overton spent a great deal of her time merely listening.

"Would you like to walk to the ballroom with me?"

She stood. "I was considering taking my nap early."

"Did you not sleep well last night?" I asked. "Is your bed uncomfortable?"

"No, no, it is nothing like that. I got caught up chatting with Daniel last evening and we did not make it to bed until late."

So he had gone back downstairs to Mrs. Overton after checking on me. Was she aware he had made that particular errand?

We parted ways at the base of the stairs and I walked down the corridor and through the doors to the left of the foyer.

Light poured in through the tall, rectangular windows on the opposite wall and lit the polished floor. A raised platform sat at one end of the room for the instruments. I could almost hear the music already, and see my country neighbors in their finest, grouping into corners and lining up to dance. I began to sway to the music in my head, my imagination importing the people from my youthful first Season, when I had danced and celebrated with little care in the world.

Clipping heels on the wooden floorboards alerted me to his presence, and I turned to see Daniel step through the large double doors into the ballroom. His gaze was at once magnetizing and fearsome and I swallowed before offering him a smile.

He stepped further into the room before pausing just out of reach. "Are you feeling better today?"

I nodded.

"I believe the light of day can do much to dispel apprehension," he said. "Many things which seem bleak in the darkness can be revealed as less formidable with a little light."

"This is no ghost hiding beneath my bed," I said, trying to swallow my annoyance. "I was not overreacting last night. My troubles are real, and it would cause me great distress if they became widely known."

Daniel was plainly surprised by my admission.

I panicked, for I had said too much. I moved to pass him and make an escape.

"Wait," he said. The plea in his voice compelled me far more easily than a command ever would.

I turned expectantly.

He looked stricken. "I didn't mean to offend you. I merely wished to offer my support. I clearly am unaware of the full extent of your dilemma."

A point which filled me with the utmost gratitude.

He stepped forward, his eyes imploring me. "You may trust me, Freya."

I felt suspended in time. I yearned to open my mouth and pour my troubles upon him. Yet I had spent years erecting a sturdy, protective wall around myself and it was not about to fall now. I learned the difficult way many years earlier that loving someone did not keep them from hurting me. And regardless, while I cared for Daniel, I did not love him.

"I must go," I said, my voice soft. "Tilly is meeting me in the guest rooms today to sort the linens." I walked from the room, my slippers silently crossing the floor and carrying me away from Daniel. I wished to turn back and see his expression, to try and read on his face how he felt, but I did not.

Instead, I fled to the privacy of my room and the comfort of my animals. Coco may have partially shifted her allegiance to Daniel, but she would always love me more.

CHAPTER 18

The weeks passed quickly after the initial planning meeting for the ball. Mrs. Heybourne began visiting more frequently under the guise of writing invitations and perfecting the menu. Her mother accompanied her a few times, but soon she began to arrive alone, which allowed her to stay for longer—and much more enjoyable—visits. We spent time preparing for the festivities, but often Mrs. Heybourne would wish, suddenly, for a walk in the gardens or a tour of the house. We went for rides along the estate and lounged in the morning room, letting the cats play with my yarn. The better I got to know Mrs. Heybourne, the less I feared her deliberately divulging my illegitimate status to the people of Linshire.

The two guest rooms on the far end of the corridor were completed. Daniel reminded me that we'd yet to move on to the next room, and I found more and more reasons to put him off. I could not bring myself to spend such a significant amount of solitary time with the man choosing wallpaper or rearranging furniture. The remainder of the rooms on the guest floor, as well as a few on my own, were not yet fit for company. But as it stood, I wasn't expecting company either.

"I am increasingly glad you have come to inhabit Corden Hall," Mrs. Heybourne said as we took tea in the morning room, Coco curled up at my feet in a pool of warm light. "Mother warned me to stay away, but she does not know you as I do. Her fears are often unfounded as it is." She lifted a shoulder to accompany her remark before sipping from her cup.

My hand remained suspended, my tea hovering before my lips. I took a sip and placed the cup in my lap. Mrs. Heybourne was sweet, but often tactless as well. Which was why I took care to watch what I revealed to her in the course of our friendship.

"This ball is already the talk of Linshire. Have you noticed the women at church? There's hardly been talk of anything else."

I relaxed, as I often did, at the happy idea that the ball I was throwing to introduce myself to the county was serving another duty by distracting them as well.

"Even Mr. Bryce has been given a clear pass for the last few weeks."

I perked up. Mrs. Heybourne often talked without need for answers or opinions. I was grateful Mrs. Overton had retired to her room for her nap and left us to speak freely. Mrs. Heybourne did not have the greatest decorum, but she did at least attempt to rein herself in when we were not alone.

"What do you mean?" I asked.

She turned innocent eyes on me. "You mean you do not know? Mr. Bryce is the largest piece of gossip in Linshire. He has been since he first arrived at Corden Hall."

"He has been nothing but a gentleman."

Her hand came up to slap her heart. "I never implied otherwise!" She leaned forward. "Mr. Bryce *is* a gentleman."

"Yes," I nodded. "I was aware of that." It was common for stewards to be gentlemen of fallen means; Daniel was no different.

"No, not *just* a gentleman, Miss Hurst. It is said that he used to run in high circles. He has come to Linshire because he is running away from something, and no one can quite figure out what that is."

This story sounded uncomfortably familiar; it sounded like my own.

She lowered her voice further. "I heard it from my lady's maid that he took advantage of your absence when he first arrived, demanding respect from the servants as though he owned the house. He required an office on the main floor, dinners in the dining room, and demanded he be waited on by the lower servants. He even began a horse breeding business from your stables."

Her eyes grew wider with each revelation, and I didn't have the gumption to confirm her accusations. It was all true.

But of course it was all true. Daniel was the steward—the highest ranking member of the paid household.

"If that is indeed the case, it is within his right as steward to require all of those things," I defended.

"Perhaps." She leaned back on the sofa. "But the way I heard it, he didn't demand them as the steward, he was pretending that Corden Hall was his."

Her words hung in the air between us, but I did not grace them with a response.

Mrs. Heybourne stood, unbothered by her revelation. "I must be getting home. Mother has been complaining about my frequent absences of late." She grinned, unrepentant. "I cannot wait for the ball tomorrow. I will arrive early as we discussed to stand beside you and welcome the guests."

I stood as well to walk her to the door. "Thank you for your help."

"It has been my pleasure."

I saw Mrs. Heybourne out before returning and slumping on the sofa. Cleo climbed on my lap and stretched, wiping her tail in front of my nose.

"Put that down," I scolded.

"She has no sense of personal space," Mrs. Overton said, joining me on the sofa. She rang for a servant and requested her special blend of tea. "Has Mrs. Heybourne gone home?"

Sighing, I nodded. "You've only just missed her. I propose we take an early night and rest up for tomorrow's festivities. Although, I vow I will not get much sleep."

"Are you nervous, dear?" Mrs. Overton asked, her wrinkled face pulling into concern as she tilted her head.

"Yes. I cannot help it."

"I will be by your side, and you have Daniel as well."

I felt the sudden desire to inquire on his character, but something deep within me warned me not to. I opened my mouth to ask but diverted at the last moment. "I am grateful to have you both, and Mrs. Heybourne as well."

"You are fortunate, you know," she said cryptically. "Daniel has really grown into himself since taking on the role of steward. He has found a contentment here that previously evaded him."

Harrison knocked on the door. "You've got a caller, Miss Hurst."

"Who is it?"

"Miss Chappelle," he replied.

I stood, holding onto Cleo. "I will receive her in the drawing room." I turned to my companion. "You may remain here if you'd like."

"I will not leave you alone to manage *her*, dear."

She followed me from the morning room, and I was glad she could not see the sheen in my eyes. I blinked rapidly until it disappeared and emotion had fully removed itself from my face.

Miss Chappelle stepped into the room moments after we were seated. The skirt of her scarlet riding habit was thrown over her arm, her hat placed at a jaunty angle on her head. Her dark eyes flitted around the room before resting on me, her lips pulling into a feline smile. I gripped Cleo closer, running my fingers down her back in a calming, rhythmic motion.

I had not missed the momentary disappointment that crossed her features when we entered the room. She was clearly hoping to see Daniel.

"I am eagerly looking forward to your ball, Miss Hurst. It is promising to be the event of the Season."

"I was unaware that Linshire had a Season," I said. One of the maids brought tea and set the service before me. One pot of tea was smaller and set off to the side. I assumed that belonged to Mrs. Overton's special blend and began pouring cups.

"Not in the official way that London does, of course. There are not many people in this county who leave for London during the Season, however, so we create our own social calendar."

"That is much like it is where I hail from," Mrs. Overton announced, surprising me. She did not often speak up in company. I'd never discouraged her, of course. She was simply quiet.

"And where is that?" Miss Chappelle asked.

"North of London. A small hamlet I am sure you've never heard of." Mrs. Overton smiled, then sipped her tea. She seemed to relax instantly. That was all she was going to say about the matter.

Miss Chappelle tilted her head, inquiring, "How long have you known Mr. Bryce?"

The question caught both of us off guard. Mrs. Overton recovered promptly. "Most of his life."

I watched her continue to drink her tea. I had assumed as much, but now it was confirmed, though it did not do much to explain *how* she knew him. Was she an old governess? A neighbor? Surely she was not a relation or they would share a surname. Unless, of course, she came from his mother's side.

"Do you know him well?" Mrs. Overton asked suddenly,

surprising me. She had a mask of pleasant inquiry on her face. I had no idea how she truly felt.

Miss Chappelle's smile became tight. "I would like to think he holds a certain preference—"

"Good afternoon," Daniel said, coming into the room. His smile was bland and he bowed before taking an open seat across from the sofa. "I simply cannot concentrate on business with such a beautiful sun shining through the window."

"Precisely what drew me to your door, Mr. Bryce," Miss Chappelle said, her voice suddenly silky and low.

Daniel's eyes lit up and I felt a rock drop into my stomach. "Did you ride over on Shadow?" he asked, unable to hide his enthusiasm.

Miss Chappelle's smile grew. "Of course. I find after I tasted her superiority, it is impossible to reduce myself to anything lesser." Her gaze flitted to me, and I knew at once she was referring to me, comparing horses to women.

"I fancy a ride myself. Perhaps I might accompany you?" he asked.

She stood. "I would love that."

Daniel looked to Mrs. Overton, excitement evident in his eyes. His face twitched when it landed on me and he hastily added, "Would you like to accompany us, Miss Hurst?"

I was an afterthought. In the face of riding with Miss Chappelle, I had been completely forgotten. Firmly clasping my teacup, I smiled tightly. "I would prefer to stay indoors."

Daniel seemed to sense something was not quite right, but a quick nudge from Miss Chappelle was all he needed to say farewell and follow her from the room, the sly minx. I could only hope the groom they used as chaperone would fulfill his responsibilities with expert care.

"It is such a lovely day," Mrs. Overton said when we heard the door close behind them.

"I am nearly finished knitting the booties," I said, standing. "I am going to fetch my basket and will return shortly."

I walked from the drawing room, shaking out my arms once I was removed from my companion's sight. I needed to dispel the tension I felt, and furiously knitting away at little booties to match the blanket for Rosalynn's baby was as good a way as any.

CHAPTER 19

The ballroom floor was freshly waxed and the chandelier lowered, polished, and filled with new candles. The musicians had arrived and were setting up their instruments, and the servants were preparing the drawing room with tables for refreshments.

I walked through the rooms on the main floor one last time ensuring that everything was as it needed to be. The retiring rooms were arranged and Harrison was already stationed at the front door to receive guests. I stood in the corridor out of the way of the servants and leaned against the wall.

The ball was sure to go off without a hitch. Mrs. Heybourne would be at my side to introduce the people I did not yet know, and Mrs. Overton would remain in the ballroom all evening in the event that I needed support.

It took a moment for the implications to set in, but I breathed out, realizing one true and important fact: I was not alone.

I did not have Rosalynn or Elsie by my side, that was true, but it had been years since I had really been able to rely on their company. With Aunt Georgina gone, it had been quite some time since I felt buoyed up by the presence of others. It was nice to feel that way again.

Daniel stepped from his office and came down the corridor toward me. I straightened, coming away from the wall.

"Are you nervous?" he asked.

"Whatever possessed me to throw a ball?"

He delivered a lopsided grin, displaying his dimple. "I believe it was the dancing."

"I can dance at assemblies. I needn't have gone to the trouble."

"I am grateful you did."

I narrowed my gaze. "Whatever for?"

His smile, and dimple, remained in place and I could not remove my eyes from them. His grin widened to reveal uneven, white teeth. "I sometimes miss these fantastically large parties. It is fun, is it not, to dance the night away with your friends, content in the knowledge that it is entirely respectable to sleep the following day away?"

"Yes," I agreed. "That is partially why I love to dance. It is such a release."

I had found a like soul in Daniel. The thought made butterflies dance within me. He gazed at me, his visible anticipation for the night ahead infecting me with equal excitement. Gone was the anxiety of earlier.

He bowed. "I better get in there and see if they have everything they need."

I nodded, watching him go. I had wondered if he might ask me to save him a dance. But alas, he did not. I ought not feel too disappointed yet, I supposed. The night had not even begun.

For once, I didn't try and squelch the hope stirring within me. I would be lying if I tried to pretend that I didn't wish to dance with him. By the end of the night, I just might.

Guests began arriving, and I was gratified to recognize the majority of them, so far, from visits at home or introductions in the church yard. Remembering all of their names, on the other hand, was impossibly difficult. It was a blessing Mrs. Heybourne was willing to stand beside me and assist in introductions.

Mr. Heybourne found Daniel immediately, and I watched them from the corner of my eye as they laughed and chatted on the other side of the room. Since the conversation earlier with Mrs. Heybourne regarding her reservations about my steward, I had been watching him closely—more closely than normal, that is. To say she had credible points was valid, but I wanted to disbelieve them. Surely it was not so terrible to step into a house vacant of a master and assume the role? Particularly when he laid claim to the highest rank present. Who else was to be in charge?

Mrs. Heybourne's facts were indisputable; Daniel's *intentions* left me skeptical.

Mrs. Wheeler arrived with her sister, Miss Clarke, but no brother.

"I looked forward to meeting him," I said when she made his excuses.

Her gaze flitted toward her sister, her mouth tightening. She appeared decidedly uncomfortable, and I regretted my words immediately. I had only been trying to be polite, after all.

Trying to regain a steady footing, I said, "I am glad you both could make it. I hope to be able to speak to you more later."

I was unable to decipher particularly what it was about Mrs. Wheeler that drew me to her, but I valued her kind disposition and guileless countenance. I felt that in her I could find a trusted friend, if given the opportunity to talk without making a fool of myself.

Disconnected notes punched through the air as the musicians tuned their instruments in preparation to start the dancing. A minuet was up first and I was glad to be stuck in the receiving line for the time being.

Couples formed in the center of the room, and I listened to

Mrs. Heybourne chatter with each new guest while I kept an eye on Daniel. He stepped out with Mrs. Wheeler, and the look of interest and charm on his face was enough to force me to turn away. But not for long. I greeted another guest but found my gaze drawn back to the dance floor.

Mrs. Wheeler positively shined. Her smile was genuine, and her gaze unfaltering. Whether attraction or some other force pulled the two together while they danced, it was enough to make my stomach churn.

"Widow."

I turned to Mrs. Heybourne, her proximity forcing me to jump. "Pardon me?"

She lowered her voice. "Mrs. Wheeler is a widow of war. Sad, sad business. And then to get stuck with the care of her brother. And childless, too! The woman deserves a good man, that's what I believe."

"And you believe Mr. Bryce to be a good man?" That was not what I had heard from her before.

She seemed to consider the situation. "He'll do well with the horses. He already is."

"Financial success is sufficient to be considered a good man in your opinion?" I raised my eyebrows. It was an odd line of thought. Or, perhaps not so odd when one considered a woman's job to marry. That created an entirely different perspective from which to judge men. I would like to think I was better capable of judging men for who they were, for I never considered them for their marriageable traits.

"Not entirely," she answered. "It is important, of course, but there are plenty of tyrants who have sufficient money. I suppose I do believe, however, that enough money can create satisfaction for most anyone. With plenty of money at one's disposal, one can choose to see or not see their spouse however often they'd like."

"The man, perhaps." I tried not to sound bitter. The tricky

part of being a woman unmarried and later in years was that others always assumed I was resentful of my unmarried state. It was difficult for them to see my satisfaction and gratification in life.

My eyes moved back to the dance floor and found Daniel once again, Mrs. Wheeler laughing at something he had said.

I turned back to Mrs. Heybourne, convinced she did not fully know her own mind if she was going to vacillate so easily about the character of another. "What causes you to believe Mr. Bryce is already successful in his endeavors?"

"He's sold a number of horses, hasn't he? I recently saw Miss Chappelle on her new acquisition and found myself a tad jealous. The beast was so lovely. But do not repeat those words. I would rather die than have her find out I wanted something of hers."

"Your secret is safe with me." And it made quite a bit of sense. My shoulders relaxed as the truth of the situation settled upon them. Of course Daniel would wish to ride out with her. He likely cared for that horse before making the sale.

We spent another half hour meeting new arrivals before Mrs. Heybourne decided she was finished with the receiving line and would like to dance with her husband. I had seen him out on the floor twice with other women and he always looked to be enjoying himself. When he approached his wife and led her out to waltz, however, his joy eclipsed any that he had displayed earlier.

A ball formed in my gut, and I turned away from them. It was not jealousy of *her*, precisely, that caused those feelings within me. I was unsure exactly what they were, but I did know that much. I had refused Mr. Heybourne years before, emphatically, and I did not regret my decision.

Mr. Bowen, the man who had sat beside me at the Heybournes' dinner weeks before, approached me for the waltz.

I placed my gloved hand on his arm and followed him onto the dance floor, prepared to be swept from my feet.

He did not disappoint, entirely. The fluid motions were much the same as any I'd endured in London's ballrooms. But the spark was missing that I typically felt in the midst of flying across the floor, grasped securely in a man's steady arms and gliding to the beat of the music.

The song ended, and another began. I danced four in a row with different partners before my feet began to ache and I slipped out of the ballroom and into the drawing room for a refreshing glass of ratafia.

Miss Chappelle stood in the corridor when I left the drawing room. Her gauzy gown clung to her legs, her hair pulled up away from her face in a complicated creation. "You must be proud," she said. "You've accomplished a great feat, for your country ball is positively a crush."

"Thank you, Miss Chappelle. I am gratified by the turnout, and happy to get to know my neighbors."

"I am sure you are." She stood before me, unmoving. Her lips formed a smirk and I felt the color slowly drain from my face. It was apparent she knew more about me than anyone else in the county of Shropshire—save, perhaps, Mr. Heybourne—and it was abundantly clear she was preparing to do something about it. Either that, or she simply enjoyed staring at me.

I rather figured it was not the latter.

"Is there anything else I may do for you, Miss Chappelle?" I tried to sound strong, but I was sure she could sense my growing trepidation. "Have you enjoyed dancing yet?"

"Yes, Mr. Bryce is a fantastic waltzer."

I knew that. I had watched them when I could while Mr. Bowen spun me around the floor. Jealousy, pure and clean, rang through me, and I tried to smile to cover up my less than lady-like feelings.

"Splendid. Then I suppose I will be seeing you inside." I

made to move around her but she stepped in my way.

Her voice lowered considerably and she said, "You might want to cease in your affections for Daniel. I would hate it if you were to get hurt."

I froze. Her dark eyes were deep and compelling and I could not look away.

"Trust me, Miss Hurst. I have spent time in London, and I have a superior understanding. If you continue down this path, you will be the one left hurting."

I watched with uncertainty as she sauntered back into the ballroom. She made *understanding* sound as though she implied far, far more. What did she understand? My attraction to my steward? Or could it have been the scandal involving my father?

I was inclined to believe she was referring to my father. I was not completely aware of where my feelings lay in regard to Daniel, but whatever they were, Miss Chappelle surely could not have known about them.

An alternative presented itself and I panicked. Could I be obvious?

The war within me was steadily raging over my feelings for Daniel and what they meant, and how advanced they were growing. I was unsure of exactly what was going on between us, and furthermore, I was unclear on precisely what sort of man Daniel was.

If my indecision was apparent to Miss Chappelle, was it equally obvious to everyone else? To Mrs. Heybourne with her odd remarks on Daniel's character; or Mrs. Overton and her observations about Daniel's contentedness; or even Miss Chappelle and Mrs. Wheeler and their potential claim on him?

If you continue down this path, you will be the one left hurting.

I did not want to hurt anymore. I had hurt enough for a lifetime—my father made sure of that. My resolve hardened and with it, my heart. I was not going to be any man's novelty, and I sure wasn't going to let myself be hurt.

CHAPTER 20

My eyes fell immediately on Daniel when I entered the ballroom, as though it was their duty to search him out. I dragged my gaze away from him and his dance partner, watching the rest of the guests and searching for a familiar face. A Mr. Bowen—one of the younger ones, I believe—walked toward me. He was likely the tallest of the brothers, and I feared I would receive a sore neck if I was forced to look up at him for the duration of an entire dance.

The dancers parted and a set of dark eyes caught my own from the other side of the ballroom. Miss Chappelle's intent gaze did not shy away from my own, and she watched me with the precision of a hawk, her expression reminding me much of Jasper, the cat, languidly secure in his place in life, and *my* inability to do anything about it.

Mr. Bowen was beside me before I had the opportunity to escape. "I would be honored if you would dance with me, Miss Hurst."

I curtseyed, allowing him to lead me out. We joined the ever-moving sea of waltzers and Mr. Bowen surprised me with his fluidity and finesse. I was happy to find that his height allowed for me to look anywhere but at my partner, as my neck did indeed lean back to an unnatural degree to see his face.

My tense muscles began to relax and my eyes lazily fell on faces as we passed. They landed on Daniel and I caught his eye, a gaze so direct it startled me. It was over quickly, but the feeling he ignited remained within me until the dance ended.

As soon as Mr. Bowen released me, Mr. Heybourne stepped in to take his place. His face, as he asked me to dance, was equal parts kindness and insecurity and I took pity on his nerves, accepting at once.

The promenade for the waltz began, and I scanned the crowds for Mrs. Heybourne's face. We had not spoken of my past experiences with her husband since that night in her drawing room following dinner. I had no concerns that she felt threatened by me, but I was uncomfortable in Mr. Heybourne's arms, my mind flitting back to that fateful day in my drawing room years before.

"Are you satisfied with your ball?" he asked me.

I nodded. "Your wife was a tremendous help. I valued her assistance immensely."

"She enjoys your friendship as well, Miss Hurst."

We continued to dance, and I watched the others spinning around us, searching for the one face I could not help but seek.

"I waited quite a long time for you to come into residence."

I jerked my head toward Mr. Heybourne, my steps faltering.

He corrected me and smiled. "I do not mean to sound odd, Miss Hurst. This is not the most comfortable conversation to hold."

"Then please tell me what you mean," I said. I had dealt with learning my mother was not legally married to my father but was in fact his mistress, in a sense. I had comforted Rosalynn as she learned of her father's indiscretions. I knew of countless men who lived lives apart from their spouses, and others who were more discreet, but just as disloyal nonetheless. If Mr.

Heybourne was preparing to offer me a proposition, I was prepared to give him a set down immediately.

"I learned of Corden Hall's ownership when I arrived to take over Fairlinn Court," he said. "At the time I thought it was a cruel hand fate dealt me. I watched the pews at church on Sundays and awaited news of your arrival."

We continued to spin across the dance floor, my shoulders tense as I waited for him to continue.

"Then, as a year went by without your presence, I began to assume you were giving us time to heal and move forward. It did not occur to me until years later that perhaps you would never inhabit Corden Hall and I might be the cause."

"I did not know you were my neighbor until I met you in the street that day."

A smile grew on his lips. "With Lady Cameron. I have always liked her."

"She is easy to like," I agreed. "As is your wife."

Affection fell over his features. He clearly loved Mrs. Heybourne very much. I felt stupid for questioning him. "I am a lucky man."

"That you are."

"May I be frank?" he asked.

Had he not been frank already? I nodded, watching the spectators as we passed. I had not seen Daniel since the previous dance. I was not actively searching for him, of course. But it was strange he was gone, nonetheless.

"I appreciate you befriending Mrs. Heybourne," he said, "and I know she enjoys your time together. In the beginning of our marriage, she struggled accepting my friendships with other women. While I have since proved to her my fidelity, her insecurities are such that I did not go into detail about the extent of my past relationship with you."

"You did tell her, though."

"Of course I did. I mentioned I had courted you just before meeting her, but it did not amount to anything."

His words were honest. He merely left out his proposal and my swift denial. If I had accepted him, I would be mistress of Fairlinn Court.

"I cannot imagine you married to anyone else," I said.

"Nor can I." He smiled, looking over my head. "I suppose I should thank you for turning me down."

I grinned, unable to help myself as the song came to a close. "You are quite welcome, sir."

The evening progressed at a steady rate, but I found myself growing more and more concerned over Daniel's whereabouts. I had not seen him since before my dance with Mr. Heybourne, and while I was not overly worried about his safety, I had hoped we would be able to share a dance. The ball was winding down, two dances remaining on the musicians' list, and I was sure I would not be able to enjoy the one dance I had anticipated most in the weeks leading up to the ball.

Mr. Morris approached. "Would you care to dance with an old man, Miss Hurst?"

"I would be delighted," I said, curtseying.

When the song came to an end, I glanced to the doorway, pleased to see Daniel step inside at that moment. Our gazes locked and as the musicians transitioned to a waltz my heart began to beat rapidly in time with Daniel's quick steps.

"Miss Hurst, would you care to dance?"

I spun, disappointed to find Mr. Fehr, a man I had been introduced to earlier in the night by Mrs. Heybourne. His height was less than my own, I was positively sure of it, and his eyes had a squint to them that caused me to believe he was in need of spectacles.

I said the only thing available to me. "I would be honored."

He led me out and I sought Daniel's face, upset to find him dancing with Mrs. Wheeler once again.

Where had he been for the last hour? I could not help but feel slighted. If he had wanted to dance with me, he'd had all night to do so. He'd also had ample opportunity to request that I save him a dance before the ball even began.

I tried to enjoy the final dance of the evening, but I could not help the disappointment which laced through me. The ball was a success, of that I could not deny. Yet my two main objectives were not accomplished. I did not get to speak to Mrs. Wheeler, and I did not dance with Daniel.

I stood at the door and received farewells and bows in abundance. Mrs. Heybourne embraced me and Mr. Heybourne sent me a twinkling smile. Directly behind them, Mrs. Bennington, pinch-lipped and sour, merely nodded my direction. The Bowen family cut dashing bows, Mrs. Bowen fully glowing in their wake. Mr. Fehr sent me a wink, Mrs. Wheeler delivered a kind smile, and Miss Chappelle a saucy grin.

By the time the final guests departed, I was utterly exhausted. My shoulders were heavy and my feet ached.

"Successful evening, Freya," Daniel said upon returning from escorting Mrs. Overton to her room.

"Thank you." I turned for the stairs, ready to shed my gown and slip into bed. Daniel, to my surprise, fell into step beside me. As we mounted the stairs, I asked, "Did you enjoy yourself?"

"I did. It was a hit."

We reached the top of the stairs, and he paused. I turned toward him, and he reached for my hand. Placing a kiss on the back of my glove, he glanced at me from under his lashes. "My only complaint was that I did not get to dance with the loveliest creature in the room."

My heart pounded, but I would not listen. I slipped my hand from his grip and smiled. "Goodnight, Daniel."

I turned away from him and escaped to my room.

CHAPTER 21

Mrs. Wheeler sat on the other end of the sofa, a warm teacup perched in her delicate hand. Her pale hair was drawn back in an elegant knot and her gown, while precisely made, was of practical design.

"I was disappointed to miss speaking with you at the ball," she said.

I smiled, preparing my own tea. "It felt like a whirlwind. I intended to come find you, but the evening was over so quickly."

"Such is the way with these balls. One spends so much time dancing that there is little time left for any visiting." Her cup clinked against the saucer and she set them both on the table. "You are recently of Yorkshire, correct?"

I paused. "No, London."

Mrs. Wheeler's face screwed up, confusion marring her soft brow. "Odd, I could have sworn I'd heard Yorkshire."

"My mother resides in Yorkshire, but I never have. I've spent the last four years in London."

She nodded as though that explained the confusion. It did not clear up mine, for I did not tell many people the whereabouts of my mother. It often led to too many questions about my father.

"And where do you come from, Mrs. Wheeler?" I asked, taking a sip of tea.

"Many places." Her eyes took on a glazed look, as though she studied something far away that only she could see. She refocused on me, offering me a sad smile. "I am sure you know I am a widow. My husband died fighting Napoleon."

"I am sorry for your loss." I shook my head. "You are far too young to be a widow."

"Many of us are too young, but that is the cost of war." She lifted a delicate shoulder and I admired her strength. "I am busy and have quite a lot of demands on my time. I keep myself occupied well."

"I do not doubt it. You live with your brother and sister, yes?"

She lifted her teacup again and nodded, taking another sip. It was apparent Mrs. Wheeler suffered, and equally evident that she did her utmost to remain positive.

We continued to speak about our upbringings, discovering more similarities than either of us expected. We both grew up on sprawling estates with joyful memories and kind mothers.

"Do you miss your mother?" she asked, reaching for another ginger biscuit.

"I do, often. I have invited her to come and stay with me, but she claims she is content with her sister."

Nodding, Mrs. Wheeler said, "I do not blame her for avoiding the journey."

A knock sounded, drawing our attention to the door, and the dashing gentleman grinning there. "May I join you?" Daniel asked.

"Of course." I gestured toward the wingback chair opposite us and poured him a cup, passing it to him as he sat down.

"Did you notice how lovely Mrs. Jamison looked last evening?" I asked. "Upon my word, she was positively glowing."

"New love will do that for a woman," Mrs. Wheeler said, a small smile on her lips. She must have been remembering the early days of her own marriage. "And Mrs. Heybourne, of course, was radiant. Mr. Heybourne is a lucky man."

I caught Daniel's eye before looking down, focusing on my ginger biscuit. "I was fond of your gown, Mrs. Wheeler."

"Thank you, Miss Hurst."

Daniel was staring at me again. I could feel it. He said, "Both of you were positively lovely. I have always loved a good ball."

"Did you attend the Season, Mr. Bryce?" Mrs. Wheeler asked. "I believe you once told me you despised London."

I glanced up sharply.

"I enjoy balls, particularly when I am fortunate enough to dance with lovely ladies." He gave us both a smile. I was tempted to remind him he hadn't danced with me. "What I am not fond of, is the Fashionable World. London's elite are far too stuffy for me."

"I quite agree," Mrs. Wheeler said concisely. "I would be satisfied to remain in Linshire for the remainder of my days."

"Would you really?" Daniel asked.

I had the feeling there was a conversation being held aside from the words said aloud, that only Mrs. Wheeler and Daniel were aware of.

I sat silently, watching them for undercurrents and clues. Was there a deeper relationship here than I had imagined? First Miss Chappelle, and now this?

If nothing else, one thing was abundantly clear: I did not know Daniel's character as well as I thought. He was a sound judge of business acumen, but a mess in regard to his social life.

And to think that I had been willing to consider sacrificing my ideals for him.

I was disgusted with myself.

"Would you care to join me for an outing on Wednesday, Miss Hurst?" Mrs. Wheeler asked. "I should love to ride the hills of Corden Hall. I've heard glorious things about the view."

"I should like that," I answered.

She hesitated. "And Mr. Bryce?"

"I am afraid I will be busy Wednesday, and you will better be able to converse openly without my stifling presence."

"Oh, stuff and nonsense," said Mrs. Wheeler, grinning. "You know your company is always welcome." She finished the ginger biscuit she had been working on for the last few minutes and stood, wiping her gloves against each other. "I must be getting home. I shall arrive at ten on Wednesday, if that suits you, Miss Hurst?"

"Lovely. I look forward to it immensely."

Daniel left to ask Harrison to have Mrs. Wheeler's carriage brought around.

I stood to follow her out, placing my cup on the tray and picking up one last ginger biscuit. "I should not eat so many of these, but I cannot help it. In the kitchen, Mrs. Covey is superior in every regard."

"I quite agree. I was able to dine here with my sister and Mr. and Mrs. Heybourne some months ago and we ate the most divine beef roast with potatoes. I am not typically a fan of beef, but Mrs. Covey quite outdid herself."

I was lost for words as Harrison came to inform Mrs. Wheeler that her carriage was waiting, my stomach clenched into a tight ball. Daniel held dinner parties before my arrival?

Mrs. Heybourne's words about Daniel's behavior refused to leave my mind. Anger suddenly filled my bosom and I marched out of the room and toward the morning room. I needed to get away from Daniel before I said something I would later regret.

"Freya, I was hoping—"

I marched past him and down the corridor, my sights set on the door to the morning room.

"Freya?" he called, louder.

I made it to the morning room and around the sofa, flung the French doors open, and continued toward the steps that led down to the lawn. Footsteps pounded directly behind me and I clenched my fists.

"Where are you going with such haste?" he called from right behind me.

I did not open my mouth, fearful for what might come out. A small voice inside me forced me to accept that while I was trying to be angry at Daniel for acting above his station, the truth was that *those* actions did not actually bother me. I was a woman of means and always had been. Had I been forced into a position as governess or companion to a shrew, I would have had difficulty acting properly submissive. Until recently, Corden Hall had no owner in residence and Daniel had been forging relationships with the people of Linshire. Far be it from me to oppose him doing his part in entertaining his friends.

What *truly* bothered me was that he did not dance with me at the ball.

"Ugh!" I clenched my fists harder while my throat made an unladylike gurgling sound and my pale face warmed in response. Daniel ran a few steps ahead of me, turning to cut me off.

"You are obviously upset about something," he said.

I stopped, watching the gold flecks in his eyes shine in the sun. I hadn't noticed them before, and he was far too close to me if I was able to notice them now. I took a step back.

"Clearly," I said, my voice dry.

"What is it? Does this have to do with the marriage that upset you?"

"What marriage—oh, that." He was referring to Sophie's engagement. Well, her *probable* engagement. There was no word it had yet occurred.

"It is safe to assume the news from your friend is not what is bothering you at present, then."

"That would be a safe assumption, yes," I agreed.

"Then what is it?" His concern was evident, but what could I say? I was not going to tell the man I was hurt because he chose not to dance with me. The entire situation was ridiculous. For the first time in my life, I was allowing myself to develop feelings for a man against all my better judgement. Why should I be so surprised that my feelings were not reciprocated?

It occurred to me in that moment that Daniel was not the problem here, but I was.

"Nothing," I said softly. "I feel foolish. Really, it is nothing."

He was not convinced. He regarded me closely, remaining a step away. I could have reached out my hand and touched his cheek and the urge to do so overcame me so swiftly that I gasped, shocked by the inappropriate thought.

"We need to create boundaries," I said, surprising myself.

Evidently, I surprised Daniel as well. "I apologize if I have caused you any distress. It was not my intent."

I shook my head. I had thought Daniel's social life was a mess only moments before when in fact, it was my life that needed a steady hand to redirect my problems.

My father returned to London with his wife and daughter, taking the *ton* by storm and effectively resurfacing the scandal of my illegitimacy. Elsie was struggling with some major issue and did not feel capable of relying on me, pointing out my inadequacy as a supportive friend. I was so focused on my steward's social life that I was obsessing over every female he spoke to or laughed with and inspecting the potential depth of their relationships. And furthermore—possibly worst of all—I was falling in love with him.

Tears formed, and I squeezed my eyes closed to stem them. I was not typically a crier and the disloyal tears angered me. I did not *want* to cry, but I could no longer pretend I did not care deeply for a man who obviously cared little for me.

Well, that was not entirely true. He cared for me. He did not, however, love me as I was beginning to love him. The fact made the compassion in his eyes all the more bothersome. Frustrated, I spun away.

"Freya!"

"No," I called back. "I need to be alone."

He let me go, and I ran.

CHAPTER 22

Mrs. Overton pinched the bridge of her nose. "I have had the headache for the better part of two days now."

"Shall I call for a doctor?" I asked. I was not concerned the day before when Mrs. Overton slept until dinner. The ball the night before had tired me as well, so it was a safe assumption that Mrs. Overton required more time to recuperate. But now, I had reason to pause.

She shook her head, settling onto the sofa while I began knitting a second blanket for Rosalynn's baby, a soft green color this time. I tucked the letter I was about to read into the basket and picked up the knitting again, focusing on my stitches.

"I have not quite lived up to my duties recently. I hope you are not upset with me."

I lowered the needles onto my lap, confused. "Why would I be upset? It is perfectly natural to take naps in the afternoon, or sleep when you are feeling unwell. I would never fault you for getting the rest you need."

Silence sat thick in the room and it occurred to me I had been quite blind indeed.

"There is more going on, isn't there?" I asked.

Mrs. Overton observed me closely. "Yes," she finally said.

"Are you ill?"

She nodded, and my chest constricted. I had just gone through this with Aunt Georgina. I did not want to go through it again. I shook my head. How very, *very* selfish of me. I laid my knitting project on the basket near my feet and scooted closer to Mrs. Overton, lifting her hand in my own, much like Elsie had done for me on many occasions.

"I am here for you. You needn't fear out of concern for me."

"It will be hard to uphold my employment agreement as I grow more ill."

I tilted my head, a small smile forming on my lips. "The only reason that Daniel fetched you was to avoid scandal. Neither of us were in any jeopardy of actually causing a scandal, but we wanted a safeguard to protect our reputations. Living in this house is fulfilling your employment agreement, Mrs. Overton, and you needn't worry anymore."

She nodded, her eyes glistening. My own cheeks were burning from the implications laced through my words. It was true; we weren't in any jeopardy of creating a scandal, but alluding to the possibility forced me to blush, regardless.

"Shall I send for the doctor?" I asked gently. "Perhaps it would be best to understand what is going on so we might know how to best move forward."

"That is unnecessary, dear."

"But, if we understand…"

Mrs. Overton shook her head and comprehension dawned, bright and true. "You already knew. Before you came here."

"Yes."

What a sacrifice for her to come stay with me, instead of remaining near her friends and loved ones. "And you didn't choose to stay in your own home?"

"It is easier this way. I have lost all my income this past

year, unable to work. Daniel knew of my troubles. It was how he convinced me to leave my home. Or, that is, what he *thought* he used to convince me to leave. But I was prepared to come and spend what time I had left beside him." She stared into the distance, seeing something I could not. Her voice soft, she continued, "My sweet Daniel has done so much for me. I could not have said no to anything he asked."

"You sound as though you are his mother."

The endearing smile she gave me made my breath catch in my throat.

"I am not his mother," she said. "But I am the closest thing Daniel ever had to one. I raised him as though he was my son, though he belonged to my sister."

"You are his aunt then?"

Nodding, she said, "Yes, though we never used the title. I was his mother in every other sense of the word. I promised my sister I would protect him, and I've done my best."

I held my breath. "Protect him from whom?"

She shook her head. "It is not important any longer."

I opened my mouth to argue and then closed it again. If Mrs. Overton did not want to share, then I was not going to press her further. "What is the diagnosis?" I asked instead.

"Heart trouble," she said. "My mother had it, and my sister as well."

"Daniel's mother?"

"Yes. She was quite young when she passed. Her heart gave out. The doctor told me I was fortunate to have been blessed with such a long life and there is nothing more they can do, aside from a special tea blend which helps to soothe my pain."

My own heart squeezed at her candid explanation. I wanted to rid her of any pain. "What can I do?"

"Nothing needs doing. I am happy here, in your lovely home. I am with my Daniel, and I need nothing more." The smile on her peaceful face reiterated the truth of her words and I felt at once reconciled.

"Regardless," I said, squeezing her hand. "I am here, and I will do whatever I may to help. You need only tell me, and I will do what I can."

"There is one thing," she said.

I waited for her to continue. She seemed hesitant, and I could feel the air in the room shift.

Her gaze drew serious. "I would appreciate it if you could keep this to yourself."

"Of course. I won't speak a word of it."

"To anyone," she said.

Sudden comprehension dawned. She did not want me to tell Daniel. "But you cannot keep this from him, surely."

"I can, and I will. I choose this, Miss Hurst, and I would appreciate your support. I do not want my last few months to be tainted. If Daniel finds out just how dire my health is, he will not treat me the same. He will fawn over me, and concern will consume him. I do not want that for my final memories."

Though I understood her reasoning, I did not agree with it. "I will keep your secret, Mrs. Overton, but I do not like it. Daniel would want to know. He deserves to know."

Her expression was kind, but immovable. "In this case, I must go with my gut."

We were at an impasse. I had made a promise, and I intended to keep it, but I was not happy about it at all.

"Can I get you anything now?"

"No dear, dinner will be ready shortly. I will be fine to wait until then."

Silence fell over us as I picked my knitting back up and resumed working on the baby blanket. The stitches became mesmerizing, and I added row after row while considering Mrs. Overton's health, and recalling the months prior to Aunt

Georgina's demise. If I had not known Aunt Georgina was sick, would I have better appreciated the time I spent with her?

I did not know; it was impossible to know. And regardless, it did not change anything here.

We separated to change for dinner, and when we came together again it was with Daniel in the dining room. I was quiet throughout dinner as I contemplated the recent change of events. It was a blessing, perhaps, that Daniel and I had experienced the row in the garden the day before, for my quietness was not out of character and thus he had no suspicions.

When dinner was complete, I begged them both a good evening, retrieved my letter from where I had stashed it in my knitting basket, and retreated to my room to read it.

The last time Rosalynn had written was to inform me about Sophie and send me the newspaper article depicting the resurfacing of my illegitimacy scandal, so it was not unreasonable for me to worry about what she could possibly have said in this letter. I had put it off for the better part of the day, however, so it was time to take a deep breath and dive in.

I sat on the edge of my bed near the lamp, unfolded the parchment, and read.

Dearest Freya,

I hope this letter finds you in good health. I am happy to report that I have given birth to a large, healthy baby boy. Once again, I have a boy! One would think I was positively heartbroken, for indeed, I did pray heartily for a little girl. But I simply had to take one look at my sweet little David Alexander and I was completely smitten. Jack does not believe me capable of having a girl. He has told me I am receiving retribution for all of those years I refused to marry him.

I believe (just between you and me) I am being blessed with

boys because I might raise them right, to treat women with the respect and dignity they deserve.

But I digress. I would love to come and visit you. I should be right as rain within a week and plan to arrive on Friday next. If that does not suit, then you need only to write and I'll change my plans. But I have tired of London and home is calling once again. The boys need room to run and I miss my damp and dreary castle.

On another note—Sophie Hurst has become engaged. She will become the Countess of Melbourne very soon and your father seems happy with the arrangement. I will not bore you with details, but I wanted to keep you informed. Much of the gossip regarding your birth has diminished. There are still the odd comments here and there, but they are from the old snobs, and we don't care much for their opinions anyway.

I hope this letter finds you well. I am sad I could not make it for your ball, and I cannot wait to hear every detail the moment I descend upon you with my horde of children.

I know you love them; you may not deny it.

All the best,

Rosalynn

I lowered the letter in my lap and lost my gaze on the wallpaper opposite. The idea of Rosalynn visiting was as tiresome as it was exciting. I did love her family, and I adored her boys. But Rosalynn had the skill to look at my face and read my thoughts and I was not in a position where I particularly wished for her to know my mind.

I sighed, lying back on the bed. There was nothing for it. I simply had to sort out my own mind and come to amicable terms with what I discovered so that when she arrived, there would be nothing left for her to puzzle out.

CHAPTER 23

Breakfast Wednesday morning was quiet. Mrs. Overton slept late, as she did most days now, and Daniel was enthralled by the newspaper he'd borrowed from Mr. Heybourne. I was anxious, due to the newspaper, and was hoping I'd be able to read it when he finished. I needed to check for any mention of me or my family in the gossip articles.

I now understood how Elsie felt all those years ago. To be discussed so brazenly was not amusing in the least.

"You have your ride with Mrs. Wheeler today, yes?" Daniel asked, startling me.

I dropped my fork on my plate and the noise clanged through the room. "Yes, we are riding later this morning."

He looked amused, an expression I had not seen on him in some days.

"What is it?" I asked, my voice curious.

His smile grew. "You've got a bit of jam on your chin."

I hurriedly wiped it away, my cheeks growing hot under Daniel's unrelenting gaze.

"You know," he said, his tone playful, "your hair becomes brighter when you blush."

"Not possible," I argued, tucking a loose lock behind my ear.

"I think it is. It must be the rosy hue to your cheeks, but every time you blush your hair undoubtedly becomes brighter as well."

A smile formed on my lips, regardless of how hard I fought it. "Daniel, you are being ridiculous."

"I will be ridiculous all the time if it results in that smile, Freya." His tone was soft and firm, and I stilled at once, unsure of what he was implying. His gaze became fervent and I could not tell for sure, but it felt like he leaned closer. "I have not been satisfied these last few days. No, if I am being completely honest, it has even been a few weeks."

I swallowed, afraid to speak up. He continued. "I have felt, recently, that a wall has been erected between us. I appreciated our easy discourse before you arrived at Corden Hall, and your frank honesty. I felt, then, we had a bond, and it only strengthened upon our meeting. But in recent weeks, I have watched you pull further and further away and it saddens me. What's worse, I cannot do anything about it for I do not know the cause. I do not know what I've done to offend you."

"You've done nothing to offend me, Daniel."

"Then what is it?"

I shrugged. "Nothing, I suppose. My own troubles have taken over every spare space in my mind and left me no room for anything else."

"That is not good enough for me, Freya. Where is the woman that wrote me detailed stories about her cats?"

I laughed despite myself. "You would like me to tell you about the cats? You see them as often as I do. You probably see Coco even more. I've noticed that she's been missing from her room the last few nights."

"She won't leave me be," he said, though his facetious smile gave him away.

I grinned. "And you enjoy it, don't you?"

"I certainly enjoy this."

My smile faltered, my eyebrows knit together. "Daniel, what could you possibly mean by that? What are you implying?"

I'd caught him off guard, that was clear. He reared back slightly, his face a mixture of uncertainty and surprise.

I stood. "If we cannot speak plainly, then there is no sense in speaking at all."

His eyes bore into me as I walked from the room, but I did not regret my words.

I met Mrs. Wheeler outside. She looked brilliant in a plum riding habit, her hair in a sleek knot and a black hat set securely on her head. Sitting atop a speckled gray mare, she was positively stunning.

"Where shall we go?" she asked as I led my borrowed mare into the yard. I had yet to purchase a horse of my own, but Daniel was kind enough to lend me his.

"I have wanted to look in on some of the northern tenant farms. Shall we go that way?" I was sure Daisy was well in Mr. Tomlinson's yard, but it couldn't hurt to check on the goat again.

"Splendid."

We rode through the wheat fields and past the wood. "I am told there is a lovely creek within those woods," I said.

"Shall we venture to find it on our way back?"

I agreed, and we continued toward the northern section of my land. I had not been that far from the house since my first tour with Daniel. Even with Elsie and Lord Cameron, we did not venture to the very edges. Mrs. Wheeler was a fine horsewoman. Secure in the saddle and in her composure, I envied her slightly.

Shaking my head, I pulled around. We'd passed Daisy earlier chewing lazily in her own yard. Mrs. Tomlinson hadn't been outside, but the goat appeared well enough to me. "To the creek?"

"Perfect."

We didn't have much room for conversation with our speed and distance, but as we came upon the wood, we slowed the horses, moving to single file on the thin path through the trees. We found the creek and dismounted, tying our horses to a branch.

"I have wanted to discuss something of importance," she began, leaning down to pick up a small stone. She watched the stone rather than my face, turning it in her fingers, a small crease appearing between her eyebrows.

Concerned, I stepped closer and laid a hand on her arm. "You may confide in me."

She looked up, a pained expression taking root. "I know we haven't known each other long, but I have always valued my own ability to discern true character, and I find you trustworthy."

I nodded, unsure of her intent. Dread gripped me and I sucked in a breath. "Are you in danger?"

She smiled softly, relieving me of my fear. "No, nothing like that. I am simply in an uncomfortable position. My brother, you see, is unable to care for us. And my sister is in need of a Season if she is going to have any luck at a match. I've received an offer from a man I knew before I married Mr. Wheeler. I have written, agreeing to consider the marriage, but his mother would like us to have a more recent acquaintance before final decisions are made. I find that I need some support. I must marry, as I have no other options available to me, but…"

"I see." I searched her face but found it void of guile. From the beginning, I felt that Mrs. Wheeler was of good character. My jealousy could only be attributed to my own poor sense. It did not reflect on Mrs. Wheeler in any light. "Have you considered asking Mr. Bryce?"

"I would not do that to him. I am grateful for his friendship, but that is all there is between us."

A swoop of relief fell over me, and I smiled despite my attempt to remain neutral.

"I wonder," she continued, "if perhaps there is another woman he has his eye on."

"Who?"

She looked away, laughing softly and shaking her head. "You are either humble or blind, Miss Hurst."

What did she mean by that? Obviously, I could deduce the general idea of her words, but I did not want to give myself false hope. I said, "I am neither. But I can honestly say there is not anything of that nature developing between Mr. Bryce and myself. He has been too hot and cold by half."

"Take it from me. Most men do not even know what they want. If you have strong feelings, then make them clear to him. Playing games will only lengthen—and potentially ruin—any chance of happiness you might have."

"I have never considered marriage to be my chance for happiness." I likely sounded more affronted than I meant to, but this mattered to me greatly.

She tossed her stone into the creek and bent to pick up another. "That is good. Even in a love match, marriage is not always happy. If you make that choice, you must be positive you love him for that is what you may fall back on when the seas turn stormy. And trust me, at some point they are bound to."

Mrs. Wheeler just delivered the most concise description of marriage I had ever before heard. I looked at her closely. "Does this apply to your friend in London?"

She cast her eyes down. "I have agreed to come and meet his family at a house party next month. I was hoping my sister might be able to come and stay with you for the duration. It is meant to last three weeks."

Surprised, my mouth fell open slightly.

She looked worried. "You are not keen on the idea."

"No, I would love to have Miss Clarke to stay. I am merely surprised you've asked me."

"I was concerned you would be offended," she said sheepishly.

"Far from offended," I explained. "I am honored."

The grin which stretched over her mouth was radiant. Mrs. Wheeler must have carried heavy burdens, for I hadn't realized how tensely she held herself before.

"You cannot imagine how relieved I am to get this sorted. I must leave in a fortnight, and I have yet to tell my sister about any of it."

"Consider this settled. Shall we return to the house? I have it on good authority that Mrs. Covey is preparing a luncheon for us."

Mrs. Wheeler grinned, tossed a stone into the creek, and wiped her gloves against each other. "That sounds wonderful to me."

I considered the components of Mrs. Wheeler's story that she had not expounded upon and determined I would do my best to support her and her sister. What I could not remove from my mind, however, was her sound argument about the institution of marriage.

I had long held the belief I was doing myself a favor in remaining unwed. The possibility that marriage was not always perfect was evident to me in not only my parents' marriage, but in those of my dear friends. Each time I witnessed Elsie and Lord Cameron bicker, or Rosalynn and Lord McGregor disagree, I convinced myself I was better off than them because I had no one to answer to but myself.

I had not considered the idea that I could be happy within a marriage while admitting it did not have to be perfect. I took myself to the French doors in the morning room and my hand fell from the handle, the rain streaming down the doors a barrier between my hedge-protected fortress and the house.

There was no roof to the garden. If I ventured outside, I was sure to become soaked before I even reached the garden gate.

I sighed, my shoulders dropping. I heard footsteps enter the morning room and knew before I turned my head they belonged to Daniel.

"The storm appeared from nowhere," he said, coming to stand beside me. We stood, shoulder to shoulder and watched the rain. "Did you see any signs of it on your ride earlier?"

"No, but I was not paying much attention to the clouds when the sun shone so brightly."

"I find I ignore the clouds as well when the sun is bright." His tone implied he spoke of much more than the weather.

I turned, sighing, then repeated my earlier admonition. "Daniel, I do not appreciate innuendos. Either speak plainly to me or cease to speak at all."

His eyes were serious and I sucked in a breath. "I do not know how to speak plainly," he said quietly. "I am not a man with a talent to express myself. I have never been able to clearly speak my mind. How do I tell you that I have been able to think of little else since you arrived at Corden Hall? How can I say, without fear of rejection, that yours is the face I search out in a room full of people?"

My breathing became shallow, and my heart battered against my chest. I knew precisely how he felt because my feelings walked the same path. What I had that Daniel lacked, however, was a fear so great that I refused to give credence to those feelings. It occurred to me as swiftly as I had felt the blossoming potential of love that it would never be possible. I could never marry, especially not this man for whom I cared so deeply.

I could not shackle myself to him, tying him to all my scandals and baggage. I didn't know all the details of his life, but I knew he'd been through enough on his own that he deserved better than what I could offer him. He deserved a wife who was not illegitimate.

Warm tears rolled down my cheeks and I shook my head, unable to speak the words that pressed against my lips.

His hands gripped my shoulders, his thick eyebrows pulling together in concern. "What is it, Freya?"

I shook my head, unable to speak.

"Freya, please. Tell me what it is."

I sobbed, a loud, horrid sound escaping my lips. Stepping from his grip, I continued to shake my head. "It can never be, Daniel."

He reached for my arm. "Do not say that—"

I tore myself away. The tears coming so quickly that I could not see him clearly. "Hear me, for I do not want to speak about this again. Daniel, it can *never* be."

I ran from the room, escaping the fears and sorrows that surrounded him. My heart tore, and I tripped on the staircase, banging my knee against the wooden ledge. I bit my tongue to keep from crying out, and pulled myself up, climbing the stairs at a safer pace, clinging to the bannister as I walked.

I entered my room, closing the door and locking it behind me. Climbing under the covers, I curled up, pulling my knees to my chest. There, in the safety of my room, I opened my heart and sobbed.

CHAPTER 24

After I cried every tear available to me, I slept through the remainder of the day. I requested a tray in my room for dinner and continued to sleep through breakfast the following morning. My head pounded from the exertion of emotion and I had Tilly create a softer knot at the base of my neck as she dressed me for the day. The looking glass revealed spotted cheeks and puffy, red eyes—I would not be able to hide my show of emotion.

But neither did I need to. Tilly informed me upon waking that Daniel left before dinner the night before. He did not inform anyone where he was going but stated some business he needed to take care of and fled.

He did not mention a return date, either.

I did not cry when Tilly told me he had left. I had no tears left to give. My heart was hardened in the night, encased by a wall so thick that nothing Daniel could do would ever penetrate it again.

I found Mrs. Overton in the morning room before lunch, her face drawn and pale, her eyes glassy.

"How do you feel?" I asked, coming to sit on the sofa.

"Well enough."

I reached for my basket of knitting supplies, but I did not feel the desire to knit. Rosalynn's sweet baby boy already had two blankets and a pair of booties awaiting his arrival. I needed to distract myself, however, and supposed I could begin a hat to accompany the booties. I pulled yellow yarn from my basket and held it limply in my hands, looking at the wool that would cover a baby. Rosalynn's fifth.

I shuddered, feeling the need for fresh tears, but none came.

Mrs. Overton spoke, causing me to jump. I had forgotten, for a moment, that she was beside me. "Do you want to talk about it?"

I looked at her then and kind, intelligent eyes gazed back at me.

I shrugged. "I do not know if there is anything left to say."

"There may be nothing new to say, perhaps, but unburdening your troubles always helps you stand easier."

I gathered a deep breath before blowing it slowly through my lips. "What do you know already?"

"Daniel only told me that there is a horse in London he has been wanting to look at, and he's been putting it off for a few weeks now. I could tell he was deeply troubled. He went to clear his mind, I am sure. You could both use a good deal of space, I believe."

Mrs. Overton was wildly observant. She obviously could see the larger issue and was offering her support. Sure, I paid her for her services as a companion, but I believed she was coming to me as a friend. Furthermore, I knew I could trust her.

I released a shuddering breath. "It will never work. There are larger things at play here, things that Daniel could never know and possibly never forgive." I glanced away, my voice growing softer. "Even if he chose to weather the storm with me, I could not do that to him. I could never ask him to give up his social standing for such a small thing."

"Your heart is no small thing."

I smiled despite my sorrow. "I was referring to marriage."

Mrs. Overton chuckled; the sound a balm on my weathered, broken spirit. "I am going to share a story now and then I shall leave you be."

I looked at her, prepared to hear the same arguments I had received countless times from my mother and other well-meaning, and sometimes not so well-meaning Society matrons.

She began. "I was married briefly as a young woman. The man was not kind, and he did not treat me well, but I had made a vow and because of that, I chose not to leave him. When I received word that Daniel's parents were both dead and the babe needed a home, I feared for his safety if he were to stay with me, so I had him placed with my neighbor.

"One night my husband did not come home. It was not so uncommon, for he liked his drink and would sometimes fall asleep in the pub or on the street. This time was different, however, and I knew within my soul something was wrong. My neighbor came to me in the middle of the night to tell me my husband had been in a brawl that evening which cost him his life."

"Oh, Mrs. Overton, I am so sorry."

She shook her head. "You needn't be. I considered it a gift from God, fell asleep and promptly went to retrieve Daniel the following morning. I may not have had much, but I have had peace ever since."

Nodding, I could not help but feel confused. If it was her intention to confirm that marriage was not a good idea, then she succeeded.

A smile tipped her pale lips. "I can see you do not follow. I was grateful for my husband. If I was unwed, I couldn't have taken Daniel in at all, for I would not have had the home and income my husband provided for me. It seems odd to be grateful for my trials, but each of them built me up to become the strong, independent woman I needed to be, for Daniel's sake."

"He was fortunate to have you."

"And he would have likely done just as well with my dear neighbors had my husband survived and I never went to claim him as a babe. The idea that we only have one clear path is not one that I subscribe to. There are many good choices, each of them worthy in their own way. What you must do is decide which path you are meant to take and then do not look over your shoulder. It does not heed one to constantly consider the past, for then we have no clear view of the future."

I looked toward the French doors that opened to the garden. Nodding, I stood. "I am going to walk outside and clear my mind. Thank you, Mrs. Overton. You have given me much to consider."

Whether she responded or not, I did not notice. My feet led me outside to the garden entrance and I opened the iron gate, stepping inside and pausing. Two paths lay before me. If I walked to the left, I would be led straight toward the hidden oasis. Right, on the other hand, would detour me through the roses and past the fountain depicting a couple dancing.

I wound my way through the path to the right, passing rosebuds tipped with dew. The fountain did not seem as horrible to me anymore, and I sat on the ledge, dropping my shoulders.

Mrs. Overton was a wise woman. It did not matter, perhaps, which path I chose, for either way I would someday end up in my own oasis.

But did I want to take the straight lane, or wander through the roses first?

CHAPTER 25

Rosalynn arrived with her family in tow on a crisp, clear morning. Much of the previous week had been laden with rain and the occasional thunderstorm. The heavens had parted and were grieving with me, for Mrs. Overton had allowed me a fresh perspective and with it, I had made a decision.

"Elsie should not be too far behind us," Rosie said, coming toward me with a glowing countenance. Her sons exited the carriage behind her and ran to me, exclaiming all at once, while a maid behind them carried a small blanket-wrapped bundle.

"Boys!" Lord McGregor commanded from atop his horse, and they all fell into line, one of the younger twins dawdling toward the front door of the house. Their father jumped down from his steed and came to stand beside his wife.

"Good day, Miss Hurst. Thank you for putting up with the lot of us."

I couldn't help but grin at his disparaging words. It was apparent he did not mean them. "You lot are welcome here any time. Come inside and Mrs. Lewis will show you to your rooms."

"Is there a nursery, perhaps?" Rosalynn asked.

I nodded, turning for the door. She walked beside me. "There is. My maids have removed the dust this week. I'm afraid it is a little outdated, but it should suit for the time being."

"Thank you, Freya. You are such a gem."

I informed Mrs. Lewis of the additional impending guests and Rosalynn and her family were led away, their servants unloading trunks and bags and carrying them upstairs to the newly renovated guest rooms. I took myself into the drawing room and ordered tea, awaiting Elsie and her husband.

Voices reached me from the foyer and I crossed to the corridor. I rounded the corner and stilled, my gaze falling on the last man I expected to see. A few days ago, I'd given up waiting for him to return. Now, however, I felt unprepared for the wash of emotions that flowed through me from simply hearing his voice.

A knock came at the door and Harrison stepped forward to open it, allowing Elsie and Lord Cameron entrance. I watched from afar as Harrison made proper introductions. Elsie glanced over Daniel's shoulder and her face lit up.

"Freya!" she called, excusing herself from Daniel and her husband and scurrying down the corridor to embrace me. I felt her cool hands come around me, pulling me tight against her, as Daniel looked over his shoulder and caught my eye.

As soon as he looked at me, he glanced away again. Saying something to Lord Cameron, he turned toward us and began walking down the corridor, his gaze on everything but my face. Anticipation skittered over my limbs as Elsie pulled away and I watched Daniel closely as he came toward me.

Offering me a small, emotionless smile at the last moment, he turned down the corridor and let himself into his office.

Crestfallen, I spun for the drawing room. "Please come in and have some tea," I said over my shoulder. I was glad my emotions did not make themselves clear in my voice. Or so I hoped.

"It was wicked of us to come unannounced," Elsie said, "but we just couldn't resist."

"You are welcome here any time, which I believe you know very well."

She dropped onto the wingback chair opposite me. "Yes, I may have assumed."

I heard Lord Cameron speaking to Lord McGregor in the corridor before they came into the drawing room, bowing and delivering proper greetings.

Rosalynn flounced into the room behind them, coming to sit right beside me with her new baby in her arms. "Isn't he lovely?" she asked.

She tipped her arms to give me a better view and I pulled the blanket away from his face. He scrunched up his little nose, squeezing his eyes closed and turning away from me. My heart squeezed, and I could not help the emotion that displayed itself in my eyes.

"He is beautiful," I agreed.

I glanced up and caught Elsie watching us, her face a mixture of love and grief. "May I hold him?" she asked.

Rosalynn passed her son to his aunt before settling herself on the sofa, Lord McGregor coming to sit beside her. I watched Elsie hold little David, gazing at him with love and longing.

Mrs. Overton came into the room and I stood at once. "Please come and sit down," I said. Lord Cameron shot up and moved toward her, offering his arm before escorting her to the seat he had occupied. He took the smaller chair to the side and leaned back, his ankle coming to rest on his knee.

"Mrs. Overton," I said, "please let me introduce my dear friends. This is Lady McGregor and her husband, Lord McGregor. The baby there is their son, David, and holding him is Lady Cameron Nichols, and her husband Lord Cameron Nichols."

I paused on Lord Cameron. He watched his wife with such love that I wanted to get up and flee the room. It was unfair that such a deserving couple would remain childless. It was not right.

"I have planned a picnic for tomorrow," I said, trying to distract myself. "I hoped we could walk to the wood. There is a charming little creek nestled into the trees and I'm sure the boys will find all manner of frogs and other slimy creatures."

"That sounds splendid," Lord McGregor said. "I have only one request."

"Yes?"

"Please force them to leave their spoils here when we depart for home."

"You mean you do not want to fill our carriage with frogs and snakes?" Rosalynn asked, affronted.

He returned her jest with a dry look and I stood abruptly, the playful banter too much to bear. I did not know why it bothered me so deeply, but it did. Five sets of confused eyes blinked up at me. "I am going to check in with Mrs. Lewis. I will return shortly. In the meantime, Mrs. Overton can help you find anything you might need."

I fled the room and turned up the stairs. I lifted my skirts and held the bannister, recalling the painful bruise I acquired when I tripped on the steps a few weeks before, the pain from that day slowing my ascent.

"Mrs. Lewis?" I called, coming upon her in the spare bedroom further down the corridor. "Do you have everything you need?"

She handed a pile of linens to the curly haired maid and came to me. "We have everything under control. There are plenty of linens and plenty of usable rooms now, so you may rest at ease."

"Wonderful." I left them to prepare the Nichols' room and slowly meandered toward the stairs, taking my time in returning. It was not right to escape my guests within minutes of their arrival and I needed to come to terms with my recent desires and file them away to consider at a later time. At the present, I needed to play hostess.

However, upon returning to my guests, I found myself fastened to the floor in the drawing room entrance, my eyes fixed on Daniel and refusing to move.

I caught Mrs. Overton's knowing gaze and snapped out of it, moving back to the sofa and sitting beside Rosalynn.

"There is so much news from Town," Rosalynn said. "I vow, this was the most dramatic Season yet."

"I believe they are all overly dramatic," Elsie said. "Which is why I've done my part to avoid them for so long."

"That is why you wanted to spend those extra months in India?" Lord Cameron asked, a smile betraying his playful words.

Elsie ignored him, smiling at a small David who seemed to be just waking up. When he began to cry, Rosalynn was on her feet at once, taking him from Elsie's reluctant arms.

"I better deliver him to his nurse," she said. "He is bound to be hungry."

Lord Cameron turned toward my steward. "Mr. Bryce, I would love a tour of the grounds if you think you've got the time."

"Was my tour insufficient?" I asked facetiously.

"Of course not," Lord Cameron answered. "I am simply looking for an excuse to beg your steward to show me his horses."

Mrs. Overton laughed. "That was all you needed to say, dear. Daniel jumps at the chance to show off his stables."

"And take the horses out for rides?" Lord Cameron asked.

Daniel grinned, and my heart turned over. "Shall we?"

The men departed at once and I was able, immediately, to relax. Daniel avoided looking my way in company, and I found myself watching him all the more for it. I had hoped when he returned we would be able to speak and put the past behind us, but it seemed he was bent on avoiding me instead.

CHAPTER 26

I led Rosalynn's boys into the wood as the servants cleaned up the remnants of our picnic. We headed down the path that led toward the creek, Elsie close behind me, Rosalynn and their husbands lagging in the rear.

"I want to catch a frog!" Harry, one of the fire-haired twins shouted.

"I'm going to catch ten frogs," his twin countered.

I couldn't help but grin when they came upon the water's edge and peered into the stream as if the frogs themselves would jump from the safety of their home, directly into their small hands. They began whispering to one another and Elsie came up beside me, holding the hand of James, the younger McGregor child.

"This place is an oasis," she said, peering at the canopy of trees over our heads.

I considered my small garden getaway. It was true—I had more than one place where I might find a little escape. It soothed my heart to think of it.

"You have a lovely home, Freya. Do you plan to remain here?"

I watched the older twins squat near the rocks, testing the water with their small, pudgy fingers.

"Yes," I answered simply. "I suppose this was not what I envisioned for myself. But I did not realize the monotony of my life in London before I came here and experienced the fresh air."

She smiled playfully. "And your father had nothing to do with that, naturally."

"I am not so prideful to admit he may have played a part in chasing me from Town, but I did not intend to remain at Corden Hall. My plan was to escape until I could assess the situation and create a plan for which to continue on."

Elsie's face softened and she bit her lip. "I fear you will not want to return anytime soon. Sophie Hurst has created quite a splash for herself. She is, I believe, the most discussed woman in London."

"*You* were once the most discussed woman in London," I reminded her.

"True. Though I did not relish it. I believe Sophie does."

We stood in silence, watching the boys play in the water. They had discovered an animal of some sort and were quietly stalking it together. I glanced over my shoulder, but the rest of the party had yet to make an appearance.

"Did you ever speak to her?" I asked, unable to help myself. My curiosity was both real and immense, and I felt all the more vulnerable for it.

She nodded. "I couldn't help myself. I wanted to know the sort of person she was."

I watched her expectantly.

"You may share a father, Freya, but I am of the opinion that your mothers played the largest role in shaping the character in each of you."

"Elsie, could you be more vague?"

She grinned. "I was trying to be courteous."

"So she is a monster?"

Her eyes widened. "She is absolutely horrid. She positively deserves attaining Lady Melbourne as a relative." Elsie covered her face momentarily with her one free hand. "But you cannot repeat that. I feel horrible for merely saying the words aloud."

"You have eased my mind, if that is any consolation," I said.

"Freya, may I speak plainly?"

"Have you not been already?"

She led Harry toward his brothers and pointed out the frog who continued to miss their darting hands. He sat beside them on the bank, enthralled, and she returned to my side. "You have more grace and compassion than most of the Fashionable World, and the *ton* was stifling your playful nature. The Freya I knew before your father's scandal has long been missing, and I have only begun seeing glimpses of her return since you've come to Corden Hall. It is perhaps a blessing you were forced into this change, for it allowed you to grow and blossom and rediscover your essential qualities, however difficult that might be to admit."

"I will readily admit it," I countered. "But I largely attribute it to Linshire's lack of knowledge. If they knew the details of my birth, I would likely be in the same state I was in London. I honestly do not know what I will do if the truth becomes known."

"You will adjust," Elsie said firmly.

I laughed without humor. "You make it sound so easy."

Her voice was soft. "It is *simple*, not easy. My life has not gone as planned. I did not intend to wed, but then I fell in love, and I adjusted. Now we have no children when I long for them, and still I must adapt further. We cannot predict the direction our life will take us, but we can do our best to take the variations as they come and…adjust."

I reached for her hand, hoping to convey encouragement and comfort.

She looked at me, emotion in her eyes. "You must understand it is acceptable to adjust to the possibility of love."

I released her hand, retraining my gaze on Rosalynn's children. "There is no need, Elsie. I already know I love him."

Her small gasp was audible. I continued, "But it means nothing. I will not drag his name through the mud."

"What name?" she asked. "He is a steward. He does not have any connections to speak of, and he has himself stated within my hearing his wish to grow his horse breeding business. The man does not have any designs on a high rank in the Fashionable World."

"You know as well as I do that all of that matters little to me. But where will he be without his good name? Who will buy his horses if he is married to an illegitimate woman?"

Her silence was telling.

I glanced again over my shoulder. "Perhaps I should find out what is holding them up."

I turned to go but Elsie stopped me. "Just do not give up. Never give up."

Trying to smile, I turned from her. Little did she know, I already had.

I heard barking as I left the shade of the wood, and I guarded my eyes from the sun, squinting to find the source of the barking amongst my friends. I was surprised to find Mr. Heybourne atop a horse, conversing with the missing portion of our party. His dog, Tiny, the large, black, furry beast, was running about the hills joyfully barking, Rosalynn's other younger twin, Lachlan, squealing in delight.

"Miss Hurst," Mr. Heybourne called, "I was making my way to meet Mr. Bryce and came upon this lovely party. Do tell me you plan to bring them to the assemblies tomorrow evening?"

"I hadn't thought of it," I answered truthfully.

Rosalynn grinned as I approached them. "Oh Freya, it could be such fun."

Her husband, on the other hand, merely looked indulging.

"I am not certain the *entire* party shares your enthusiasm, Rosie, but I am open to the idea."

"Capital!" Mr. Heybourne said, his grin spreading. "Positively capital. I shall see you all tomorrow night. Farewell!"

He took himself off.

"Shall we find ourselves some frogs?" Lord Cameron asked, amused.

"The boys may need some of your expertise," I said.

"Very well, let us go."

CHAPTER 27

Mrs. Covey duly impressed my guests with dinner preceding the ball at the assembly room in Linshire. She must have heard about her elevated guests and did her utmost to deliver a meal fit for the aristocracy.

Upon hearing our plans, Daniel informed us about the dress code, graciously less severe than that found in Bath or at Almack's in London, undoubtedly due to Mr. Heybourne's role as Master of Ceremonies. He was, in essence, a relaxed man, finding joy in all things. Furthermore, it was evident in the company he kept that Mr. Heybourne was an understanding individual, not at all high in the instep.

We loaded into two carriages and I had the misfortune of sitting opposite Daniel, Mrs. Overton on the forward-facing seat beside me. Conversation was sparse, Mrs. Overton inquiring on my friends and the origin of our relationships.

"I have known them both since we were girls at school. Their husbands I met during our first Season in London. It was quite some time ago, but I beg you will not ask how long for I would prefer not to own up to it." I accompanied my words with a self-deprecating smile.

Mrs. Overton smiled, her fatigue concealed in the fading light. "You are fortunate in your friends. They are lovely."

"Indeed, I am," I agreed.

"Your friends are fortunate as well," Daniel said, his low voice sending a shiver up my spine. It was the first time he had directly spoken to me since returning from London.

I stared at him, lost for words. He watched me back with his mouth firmly closed, his face a work of stone I could not decipher, try as I might.

The carriage pulled up to the front door of the assembly hall. Music and laughter poured through the candlelit windows, the dancing already well underway.

The carriage door swung open and Daniel hopped out, turning to hand out Mrs. Overton. He faced me and my hand slid into his, our gazes locking as warmth spread up my arm. I felt a chill the moment he released me. Mrs. Overton walked on ahead of us and Daniel held out his arm to escort me inside.

"May I reserve the first waltz?" he asked, his voice so low I wondered if I'd heard him correctly.

I nodded, afraid that speaking aloud might break the spell.

The second carriage pulled up behind ours and I could see Elsie and Rosalynn exiting as I walked into the building. I caught Mrs. Heybourne's eye as I stepped through the door and at once felt something was wrong, for she did not return my smile, but instead shifted her gaze uneasily away.

Mr. Heybourne greeted us at the door, a strained cheerfulness about his face. "Welcome. How glad I am that you could make it," he said, his voice betraying his lie.

Daniel froze behind me. He must have sensed something was off. My gaze flitted from face to face as I tried to make sense of the discomfort I felt, aware of my friends and their husbands coming through the door to stand behind me.

I caught Miss Chappelle's calculating eye and knew immediately what was wrong. My secret was *out*.

Dread filled my body as the blood drained from my face. I felt faint at once and turned to go, but Daniel gripped my arm, refusing to let me leave.

"Let me go," I whispered.

"Do not let them win."

I looked at him, my eyebrows drawn together in confusion.

He smiled at me as though nothing was different. "I believe our waltz is beginning."

"Daniel, no, you cannot know—"

"Yes, I do," he countered. "Now please dance with me."

He swept me into his arms and I allowed him to pull me into the center of the dance floor.

Spectators created a circle around us, fans fluttering, eyes narrowed in judgment. I caught Mrs. Bennington's self-satisfied smirk and turned my face away, ashamed.

Elsie drew Lord Cameron onto the dance floor to join our set, and Rosalynn joined with Lord McGregor. Our party danced a few measures longer before Mr. Heybourne pulled his wife onto the dance floor, much to the obvious dismay of his mother-in-law.

Mrs. Heybourne refused to meet my eye in passing, but I appreciated the show of support.

Mrs. Wheeler was last, her partner a very tall, blond, Mr. Bowen—I was not entirely sure which one.

The rest of the occupants in the room remained firmly on the outskirts, observing. They had convicted me already.

"Thank you," I said. I looked into Daniel's eyes and nearly faltered at the intense heat emanating from them. He held me securely, not allowing a single misstep before the many scrutinizing faces.

"You needn't thank me."

I clamped my mouth shut. He was likely acting the gentleman, but there was no mistaking his words. *He knew*. He handed me away and I joined the women in the center of the set before the dance took me back to Daniel.

"How did you find out?" I asked, embarrassment warming my cheeks.

"It was not difficult. When I went to London there was quite a bit of talk about a Miss Hurst. It was not so difficult to connect the French Miss Hurst to you."

I nodded. I should have assumed he would hear, but it had not occurred to me, so caught up as I was in deciding whether or not I loved him.

The song came to a blessed end and Daniel grabbed my hand amidst my curtsy, dragging me from the room. He pulled me outside, in clear view of the windows of the assembly. I could see a cotillion forming, my friends doing their part to join in the dance.

"Was that the cause?"

"Pardon?" I asked, unsure of his meaning.

He glanced at the windows, then back to me, dragging a hand over his face. "You told me we could never *be* together. Was it because of your father?"

"Is that not a valid reason? Daniel, I am illegitimate. Marrying you would bring shame to our marriage and our household. You saw how quickly the people in there were willing to cut me. With my stigma attached to your name, you would never sell another horse."

"Blast the horses! You think I care more about horses than I do about you?"

A memory flashed in my mind of Daniel asking Miss Chappelle to ride out with him so he could see her horse, forgetting about me.

"I don't," he said. "I love you, Freya. I have loved you for some time now. I do not care about your father's poor choices or what anyone else thinks of us. Confound them all!"

"It is so easy for you to say that. You have not had to live through such a scandal. Friends one week cut me the next. I am reliving a nightmare." I pointed toward the assembly hall. My eyes began to smart and I blinked rapidly, trying to dispel the tears before they came.

"You only saw the judgmental, flighty onlookers," he said. "Did you notice those who stood in your support?"

I was struck by his words, my mind replaying the few who stood up to waltz despite the rumors.

His voice lowered and he stepped closer. "You are not alone. You will never be alone."

Tears rolled down my cheeks, warm and slow. My lips curved into a heartbroken smile. "Daniel, the trials are only just beginning."

"Then begin them with me."

He stepped closer, his gaze falling to my lips. My heart banged against my chest as his hand slid around my waist, the other moving to cup my jaw. He descended on my lips, lightly pressing his own to mine, until my chest burst.

Time and space became obsolete while Daniel kissed me, and comfort settled over my body like a warm blanket.

I was suddenly pulled from the euphoria by a woman screeching.

"Daniel Bryce, what do you think you are doing?" she shrieked.

He pulled away abruptly, spinning toward the woman on the street, regally standing before a crest-emblazoned carriage. Lady Melbourne. What in heaven's name was she doing *here*?

"I am getting engaged," he said, unamused. "If she'll have me." He did not take his eyes from the older woman when he said, "Freya, allow me to introduce my aunt."

CHAPTER 28

I was nearly positive my jaw had dropped to the cobbled street below me. I glanced at the illuminated windows of the assembly hall lined with shocked faces. How long had they been observing us? My cheeks burned, and I turned my back to them, though what I faced in the street was not much better.

Lady Melbourne fumed, her wrinkled face pinched with anger. "Get in this carriage immediately," she demanded.

I stepped forward to comply when Daniel shot out his hand to halt me. I don't know what I had been thinking, but she was so compelling I felt the need to obey.

"I will not go through this again, Aunt. I am not interested."

"It matters not what interests you," she said, her voice dripping with derision. "You will soon become an earl whether you want to or not. Now come with me before the whole of this pathetic little town knows all of our business."

Daniel fumed with equal intensity, the muscle in his jaw jumping as he clenched his teeth. "How many times must we go over this? I am not interested."

I did not know the details of their dispute, but I did agree that the middle of the street in Linshire was not the proper place to discuss it.

I didn't notice when Mrs. Overton joined us on the street, but she came to stand beside me, a calm, solid force in the face of such blatant animosity. "Shall we return to Corden Hall and discuss this in private?" she asked.

"That is what I have been trying to accomplish," Lady Melbourne huffed.

Daniel looked at me as though asking permission. "Of course," I said.

"I will inform your guests," Mrs. Overton said, turning back toward the assembly hall.

Daniel faced me. "We will deal with her and send her on her way. I am sorry."

"It appears as though I was not the only one holding onto a secret," I said.

He regarded me closely. "No, you were not."

The Nichols and McGregors chose to remain at the ball, giving Daniel and his aunts the space they needed to work through their disagreement. I rode home in my carriage with Mrs. Overton and a very quiet Daniel. When we pulled into the drive I asked, "Would you like us to make ourselves scarce or do you prefer support?"

He considered my question, then shook his head. "I don't know. Selfishly, I would ask you to come with me. But I would rather shield you from her wrath."

"I will not leave you, Daniel," Mrs. Overton said. "She does not frighten me."

He took a deep breath. "I refuse to be connected to them. They disowned my father the moment he married my mother and I will not become their plaything. They wanted nothing to do with me when I was born; I want nothing to do with them now."

As the details clicked into place, I tried to cover my surprise.

Daniel was Lord Melbourne's heir. "But wait, I thought Sophie was engaged to Lord Melbourne's heir."

Daniel paused. "Married," he corrected. "The wedding occurred only last week."

I was so confused by the tangle of people and relationships I did not know what to think. Clearly, Sophie Hurst had not married *my* Daniel.

"She married James Bryce," he said. "He is the next in line for the earldom *after* me. I don't know the direct relation, but he is a cousin of mine of some sort. I have been avoiding my aunt and uncle for years now and James led them to believe I was dead. Lady Melbourne hunted me down when she received word I was in London last week. Evidently, she has followed me here."

He was next in line to become an earl and didn't seem to care in the least. The man truly was a marvel. "I will do whatever you need me to do," I said.

Daniel nodded, then left the carriage, helping me and Mrs. Overton onto the gravel drive before walking into the house.

Lady Melbourne was already seated in the drawing room, comfortably set up as though Corden Hall was her home and we, the visitors. We hovered at the entrance of the drawing room doorway, allowing Daniel to take the lead.

"I will make you a deal," he said, coming to stand before Lady Melbourne, fearless and strong.

"I'm listening," she said, wary.

"I am not going to come with you now, so you may cease your attempts to convince me to move to the Abbey. I am recently engaged to marry and would prefer to enjoy my wedding free of manipulations and bribery. Leave us be, and I promise you when it becomes *necessary*, I will discuss the situation with my wife and approach you with our answer."

He had yet to actually propose to me, of course, but that was a minor detail. Hearing the words caused my heart to skip a beat, regardless. If I was understanding him correctly, he was telling his aunt he was not entirely closed to the idea of coming to her and Lord Melbourne, but that she needed to give him time to decide.

She seemed to sense the same change I did. She studied his face, her small, bleak eyes narrowing. "That is not good enough for me," she finally said. "I will not have the Bryce name dragged through the mud by any connection to her."

Her eyes shifted to me, and I felt the sting of them from across the room.

Daniel tensed visibly. "You have no right to dictate any aspect of my life."

"As matron of this family—"

"You lost any claim to call me family when you turned away my parents and refused to take me on at their death."

She straightened in her chair. "Had I known then that I was barren and you would become the next in line, of course I would have taken you in and reared you up properly."

Daniel scoffed in disgust. "You are welcome to stay here for the night, if my mistress is not opposed, but I bid you will take your leave at first light. You've received what I am willing to offer. Take it or leave it; the choice is yours."

Daniel turned and walked from the room, brushing past Mrs. Overton and me before escaping to his office down the corridor.

Lady Melbourne stood, derision dripping from her face. She speared me with a look. "Well, I *never*," she muttered, passing me. She shouted at Harrison in the foyer and I flinched when the front door slammed behind her. I was grateful she chose to leave right away. That, I could not deny.

"You should go to him," Mrs. Overton said.

"I am sure he needs a moment alone."

She turned for the stairs. "I am going to sleep." Pausing on the step, her hand resting on the bannister, she looked at me one more time. "Go to him," she said.

I watched her leave. The last few hours had brought a swift storm of emotions. I didn't have time to properly process any of it, and I was sure Daniel needed time as well. But my human needs won out and I found my feet carrying me toward his study.

I knocked lightly, opening the door after a moment of quiet. Daniel sat in a chair in front of the fire. I recognized the chair he sat in from my last visit to the office, but it had previously been sitting in front of his desk. He must have dragged it before the fire at an earlier time, for now the hearth was cold.

"Daniel?" I asked, unsure of myself.

"I am sorry," he said, the words muffled from his hands holding his face.

I crossed the room, placing my hand on his shoulder. He glanced up at me and my heart broke and soared simultaneously. I felt an overwhelming surge of emotion for this man, my eyes brimming as a result.

He was on his feet immediately, pulling me into his arms. "Do not cry," he said softly.

"I cannot help it," I whispered back. "I am so happy, yet so terrified at the same time."

I could feel the chuckle reverberating from his chest. He pulled back and looked at me. "Can we make an agreement right now?"

"I suppose that depends on what it is."

Smiling, he pulled me toward him again. "Can we please get married?"

"Oh, Daniel, I thought you would never ask."

He pulled me closer, kissing me softly, his lips warming mine with their smooth touch. My chest burned with love as I gripped his coat, tugging him closer, allowing his love to ease my trepidation. When he backed away, he smiled, his dimple making a delicious appearance.

"What are you going to do about the earldom?" I asked, a

little concerned. I had not signed up to become a countess. I was not sure I was even up for the job.

He lifted a shoulder. "I am not going to worry about it until I need to."

"But I was under the impression Lord Melbourne is nearing the end of his life."

Daniel shook his head. "The tyrant could live another ten years for all I know, or care. I am not going to bother myself with any of it until it's staring me right in the face. And like I told that woman, when the time comes to make a decision about where we shall live, *we* will decide together."

I nodded, but I already knew where I stood on the matter. This was an issue that had affected Daniel and his parents for the entirety of his life, and part of theirs. It was not my decision to make. I already planned on supporting him in whatever path he chose.

I had written off my father and his new family and did not regret my decision. If Daniel was willing to stand by me throughout the peril that awaited and the scandal that Miss Chappelle had recently opened within the parish, then I was going to do the same for him, no matter what.

"I suppose I can move back into the house soon," he said facetiously.

I grinned. "Not until after the wedding. But it is probably a good thing Coco loves you so, for she has already claimed the bed in the master's suite. I hope you do not mind a dog to warm your feet."

"For you, I'll put up with anything."

CHAPTER 29

Mrs. Overton requested a breakfast tray in her room so I checked on her that morning, concerned for her after the eventful night before. She was no worse, only tired, and said as I was leaving that she would allow me to tell Daniel of her illness.

I hovered at the end of her bed. I planned on sending him up to speak with her after my guests departed, but I could not remove the worry from my heart. If she was willing to tell Daniel, then it was probable her time was coming—an eventuality I was not prepared to face.

"Fix that long face, dear," she said with kindness. "It is not as bad as you are assuming."

"Then why have you changed your mind about telling Daniel?"

She glanced to the window before responding. "Lady Melbourne's return forced me to reconsider. If Daniel is refraining from any connection to her because of me, I want him to know that I am fine with it before I go. Besides, he deserves to know."

I nodded. "I don't understand why Lord and Lady Melbourne

want him to come to them anyway. Daniel said himself that the present earl could live another ten years."

"Yes," she agreed, adjusting herself on her pillows. I hastened to help her, sitting myself on the edge of her bed. "But Lord Melbourne has spent his life building up his home and lands and political seat. It is only natural for him to wish to pass on his knowledge and customs to the heir."

I hadn't considered that perspective before. Had Daniel?

"Do not fret," Mrs. Overton said sleepily. "It shall all work itself out in the end."

I leaned forward to kiss the woman's forehead before letting myself from the room and leaning against the door. Her words stuck with me and I could not help but think of the importance of posterity. I did not blame Lord Melbourne for having the desire to pass something on to future generations.

Carrying myself downstairs, I sat at the breakfast table, surrounded by my two closest friends, their husbands, and my Daniel. But I could not remove the conversation with Mrs. Overton from my mind.

"You will let us know the moment you set the date, yes?" Rosalynn asked, pulling me from my musings. "I must be here."

"I will let you know," I agreed.

Elsie simply watched me, a continuous smile on her face. It was unnerving, but I imagined my mother having much the same reaction.

"We will have to wait at least a month," I told them. "I am having a guest come to stay soon, and she will remain a few weeks at least."

"You have not told me this," Daniel said.

"Have I not? Mrs. Wheeler asked if we could have her sister, Miss Clarke, come to Corden Hall while she attends a house party. I told her I would be delighted." An image came to my mind of the scene at the assembly hall. "Unless, of course, she's changed her mind."

"She stood up last night," Daniel reminded me, referring to the waltz at the assemblies. It was true. Mrs. Wheeler was one of the select few who chose to support me in the face of adversity.

"Perhaps we shall have everyone to stay at our castle for Christmas," Rosalynn announced. "Wouldn't that be splendid fun?"

"Capital, darling," Lord McGregor said indulgently.

Lord Cameron sighed. "It is settled then. We will all freeze to death in the McGregor castle for the holidays."

"It is not so drafty when you grow used to it," Rosalynn defended.

"Of course not," Elsie said, grinning. She turned to Daniel. "We shall have a splendid time. Just do not forget to bring extra warm cloaks."

Their carriages were packed and filled with small boys—sans frogs, of course—and we gathered in the drive to say our farewells. I was proud of myself for keeping a dry eye as I waved to the disappearing carriages. I had cried enough within the last month to fill my quota for the year.

"Shall we?" Daniel asked, offering me his arm.

I clung to him, walking toward the house. "I am glad you get along with them. They mean a great deal to me." Elsie and Rosalynn were the family I could rely on.

"They admire my horses. What more is there to like?"

"Yes," I said with a laugh. "What more, indeed?"

He led me into the foyer and I pulled back on his arm. "Mrs. Overton would like a word with you in her chamber."

Confusion marred his brow. "What is it about?"

I drew in a breath. "You will have to speak with her."

He turned to go but I spoke, forcing him to turn back. "Will you regret the opportunity you have now to learn from Lord Melbourne?"

He stilled. "Learn what, precisely?"

"He has been the earl for years. He probably has a lot of knowledge and customs he would like to pass on to the next one. Do you know much about running an earldom?" Mrs. Overton wouldn't mind my borrowing her words. It was she who caused me to consider these things in the first place.

Daniel ran a hand over his face. "I was not planning on worrying about any of this until after our wedding, at least."

Nodding, I stepped closer and picked up his hand in both of mine. "Then we needn't worry about it. I merely wondered if it was something to consider." I sighed. "I have not wanted to admit as much, but I have not been comfortable with the way I left things with my father when I saw him last. I have been telling myself it was the right thing to do, and that I should be glad he's gone from my life, but the truth is, he did try to write me for a full year before he gave up. With a complete lack of response, how can I blame him?"

"You're hurt."

"Pain is not a valid excuse anymore. My father's abrupt arrival at a ball with no prior warning was not exactly ideal, but that is not just cause for cutting him out of my life entirely. Elsie told me once that holding onto this anger and pain would only hurt me. I can see now what she meant by that, for I pretend not to care, but I do."

He leaned forward and tucked a stray curl behind my ear, sending shivers down my neck. "What do you plan to do about it?"

Warmth grew in my heart at his touch. I would not let anything ruin the beginning of our relationship. "I am going to write to my father," I said. "I will tell him I forgive him."

Daniel nodded, his arm coming around me to pull me close. "Do you?"

"Yes," I said quietly. With his arms holding me tightly, I felt I would never want for anything.

"Then I suppose I ought to follow your noble lead."

"You shall write to my father, too?" I asked.

His chuckle vibrated his chest and sent shivers down my arms. "No," he clarified. "I shall wait until after we wed, but I will write to Lord Melbourne and accept his offer."

My breath turned shallow as realization dawned that I did not know exactly what Lord and Lady Melbourne had asked for. "What was his offer?"

"For me to move into the Abbey and learn the workings of the estate and lands."

"Forever?"

He leaned back to look me in the eyes. "No. I shall not plan to live there forever. Only long enough to get a lay for the land and then we can return here."

"We?"

His dimple appeared with his smile. "Of course, *we*. I will make it very clear that I shall only come with my wife. I have confidence they will not refuse me."

"Who could refuse you?" I said, sliding my hands up to grasp his lapels.

"You tried to," he reminded me.

Laughing, I shook my head. "But it did not last long."

"No, it did not. And for that I am eternally grateful." He leaned in to kiss me and I felt the world fall from beneath me, Daniel's arms holding me steady and secure in his embrace.

I had the distinct impression I would always feel this way in his arms, and it was an enticing prospect, indeed.

EPILOGUE
SEVEN YEARS LATER

"Harriet, come here please," I called, standing at the base of the stairs. My five-year-old held my gaze, hopping down the steps one at a time. "Your father is waiting outside and is quite nervous. We need to be on our best behavior today."

"Yes, Mama," she said, sliding her hand into mine. "I will not fuss. I promise."

I shall believe that when I see it. Pulling her toward the door, I rested my hand on my slightly rounded belly, feeling for the foot that had just pushed against my stomach. Only two more months and we could meet Harriet's little brother or sister. I had strong suspicions it was a little brother, but I refrained from voicing that opinion. I did not want to get Daniel's hopes up.

The winter air bit my skin as we crossed the gravel drive, and I rested my hand on Daniel's arm, garnering his attention. He glanced up, his green eyes concerned.

"It will all be well," I said. "You are prepared."

The footman stood at the carriage door, waiting to help us in.

Daniel swallowed. "But what if I'm not?"

My fingers tightened their grip. "You are. You spent four years learning from Lord Melbourne. And the Abbey is ours now, to do with what we please. You may redecorate it to your heart's content and make it your own. It *will* become our home."

His smile turned warm. "Indeed. As long as I have you and Hattie, I need nothing more."

"And?"

His gaze dropped, his hand resting on my belly. "And this little prince or princess." He met my eyes. "And you will not resent me for ripping you away from Corden Hall?"

Reaching up, I cupped his cheek. "You are not ripping me away from anything. The Abbey will become our new home, and we will return here to visit. I do not resent your decision to accept the mantle placed on your shoulders, and you know Mrs. Overton, were she here, would be proud of you, too."

"Come, Daddy!" Harriet exclaimed, climbing into the carriage. "We get to go to our new house today!"

"True." He leaned down and kissed me, pressing himself against me as he pulled me closer. Lowering his voice, he whispered, his voice husky. "I am so fortunate to have you."

I shot him a saucy grin before following Harriet into the carriage. Daniel settled in beside me and closed the door, rapping his knuckles against the roof. We rolled away, and I settled into Daniel's side.

"I cannot wait to begin this adventure," Harriet said, grinning.

"Neither can I, darling." I glanced back over my shoulder to see Corden Hall disappear through the back window.

Contentedness settled on my shoulders. On to the next adventure.

SNEAK PEEK
LOVE AT THE HOUSE PARTY

Chapter One

Backlit by the moon, the creeping dark fingers of the branches outside the attic window gave me a chill as their shadows inched closer to my feet. Dim light flickered on the walls of the small room as I pulled the quilt tighter around my shoulders. With no fire, it was all I could do to keep warm while my icy fingers threaded the thin needle again. Fighting my drooping eyelids, I focused on the final row of vines awaiting their leaves on the hem. The gown was near to finished and I was determined to complete it before I slept.

Pushing a yawn into my blanket-wrapped shoulder, I stitched another leaf. Only eight more to go.

Mr. Bancroft was nothing if not polite, and would surely compliment whatever I arrived to his house party wearing—be it a potato sack or an outdated ball gown. I chose to create something that landed in the middle. And yet, unease still skittered through my body. How was I to know I was doing the right thing?

My eyes sought the stairway. I would not fetch the letter to read again, no matter how strongly I felt the desire to reassure myself. Mr. Bancroft had stated very clearly that the house party was a mere formality—he anticipated his mother would admire me just as much as he did. All the same, he required her blessing on our union before we entered into a formal understanding. I trusted Mr. Bancroft, but the uncertainty left me feeling testy and unsettled. What if he found me very changed and regretted his desire to marry me? Until I received a proper proposal, nothing was set in stone.

The needle slipped through the muslin, pricking my finger. I shoved it into my mouth before a drop could bleed onto the fabric. This last gown was all I had left to complete, and I was not about to ruin the soft cream material due to careless fatigue.

The stitched leaves grew blurry as I made my way down the vine, completing the embroidery just before the shadows reached the tips of my toes. I tucked them farther under my chair, regardless. Draping the gown over the chest on the attic floor, I stood, pulling the blanket with me. The cold spring night wafted through cracks in the plaster walls and sent a chill down my spine. Another yawn interrupted my thoughts and I made my way from the attic, quietly creeping to the door of the bedroom I shared with my younger sister.

Pulling out the key, I unlocked the door, hoping the click and creak didn't wake my sister. The key had not always been a necessary precaution, but lately I had grown used to remaining behind locked doors—something that I was determined to change in the near future.

Slipping inside, I locked the door again and slid the bolt into place. Soft snoring punctuated the dim chamber and I watched Charlotte for a moment before settling under the quilt beside her. Doubt and anxiety crept away when my motivation lay so plainly before me. A house party was not ideal, yet neither was Mr. Bancroft. But one thing was certain: together, those two things had the ability to pull Charlotte and me from our current situation, and perhaps provide the potential to help our brother, Noah, as well.

If only he desired it.

Sighing, I rolled over, fatigue from completing four new dresses for the house party and a host of small adjustments to older gowns fully catching up with me.

"Eleanor?" a sleepy voice questioned from the other side of the bed.

"Hush, Charlotte," I whispered. "Go back to sleep."

She groaned. "You've been sewing, haven't you?"

I refused to respond. It mattered little that it was so late; I had a house party to attend. What choice did I have but to finish the gowns?

Charlotte yawned loud enough I could hear it in the thick darkness. Her voice groggy, I half wondered if she would remember this conversation in the morning. "Can we not find *some* little money to pay a seamstress?" she asked.

Squeezing my eyes shut, I shook my head, not that she could see. At seventeen, she could not quite grasp the desperation of our situation. "There is no need. I am finished now."

"You do too much," she said sleepily, already returning to the land of dreams.

"I love you, Lottie."

Another yawn interrupted her as she said, "I love you, too, sister."

Sleep failed to arrive, despite my exhausted state. I had one chance to pull my sweet sister from this horrible, bitter house and give her a chance at marriage. And I would do everything in my power to be successful.

The road to Bancroft Hill was fraught with rain. Pattering raindrops on the roof drummed a steady beat, interrupted by

Emma's soft snoring opposite me in the coach. With Charlotte safely at Corden Hall in the care of our neighbor and friend, Miss Hurst, and Noah clearly without need of a lady's maid, Emma was able to accompany me to the three-week-long house party. Her stone-like face accepted the duty with no complaint and I found myself grateful to bring a piece of home with me.

Pulling the lap rug tightly over my knees, I fought a shiver, closing my novel and tucking it away. The overcast sky had grown too dark to see clearly and reading about dreadful highwaymen with shocking facial scars was not particularly conducive to a relaxing ride along the highway, especially as I had yet to discover if the highwayman in the novel would turn out to be a blackguard or the hero. One never did know with gothic stories.

Lightning flashed in the distance, momentarily lighting the increasingly darkening carriage and I startled when Emma yelped across from me.

"It is only a storm," I soothed. "It won't be much longer to Bancroft Hill. We should be fairly close by now, I'd imagine."

She nodded, her round eyes betraying her younger years. She had only come to work for us the year prior. I had quickly promoted her to lady's maid when she'd displayed a superior talent at styling my thin, straight hair into something resembling elegance. The pale locks had long been the bane of my existence. While my hair was a lovely shade of light blonde, it was impossible to curl and rarely held a style for longer than a moment. But Emma was a master. I looked better under her care than ever before.

"Shall we play a game to pass the time?" I asked.

Emma's confused eyebrows pulled together slightly. "What sort of game?"

Before I could answer, a sudden jolt threw me from my seat. A blow reverberated through my jaw as it collided with Emma's knee, shaking both of us as the carriage shuddered to a stop.

"Mrs. Wheeler!" Emma shrieked. "Are you hurt?"

"I shall survive." Rubbing my jaw, I regained my seat. The door flew open and rain poured sideways through the door, instantly soaking my feet through my soft leather shoes and traveling up the hem of my gown.

"Nasty storm out here, ma'am," Joe, my coachman, said.

"The roads have turned immovable?" I guessed.

His sorry face nodded. "Hit a rut back there that cracked the wheel." He closed the carriage door enough to keep out some of the rain. "A carriage has been following us for a while. I'll flag them down and ask for help."

"Thank you, Joe."

Forcing the door shut with a click, he left us in the relative warmth of the cab. I tamped down my frustration. If Noah had taken care of this carriage instead of wasting all of his money on cards and drink, I would be bouncing along to Bancroft Hill instead of slumped on the highway like a pair of discarded shoes.

Emma scooted closer to the opposite window, watching through the streams of rain. "There's it now."

"There it is now," I corrected.

She shot me a look over her shoulder, her eyebrows drawn together. "That's what I said."

It was senseless to attempt any sort of education with the girl. But at times her speech grated on me, and after raising Charlotte for the last few years, it was second nature to correct such horrid speech. "Are they stopping?"

"Yes'm. A man's talking to Joe."

"I best be part of this," I said, sighing.

"Whatever for?"

My hand rested on the door handle and I looked back at her. "Because I do not want Joe sending us with someone who isn't respectable. I'd rather wait here in the cold than ruin my reputation."

That seemed to quiet the maid. Fierce wind ripped the door from my hand and it hit the opposite side of the cab with a loud bang. I hopped down to the mud, gripping the slippery door and yanking with all of my strength, though it refused to budge.

Joe must be a man of goliath strength, for he had made it appear easy to hold the door partially open earlier.

I counted aloud, prepared to give the door one large yank with accumulated strength, "One...two...three!"

My arms flew through the air, the door coming away from the side of the carriage easily as though the wind had died down on my command. The hair whipping into my eyes said otherwise, however, and I turned to find a man standing directly behind me.

"Good heavens," I shrieked, my hand flying to my heart. "You frightened me."

"What are you doing?" he hollered over the wind. His coat was drenched, his hair plastered to his forehead.

"What business is that of yours?"

"You are heading to Bancroft Hill?" he asked, ignoring my question. His eyes narrowed at me through the pelting of icy drops of rain.

Joe. Of course my coachman would divulge this information to a complete stranger. A quite tall stranger, in fact, with hair so dark it could be black—or perhaps that was an effect of the powerful rain.

A flash lit the dark sky, giving me a glimpse of the stranger's face. He did not *appear* nefarious. His clothing screamed gentility and there were no visible scars running the length of his cheek. If he was a highwayman, he was *bound* to have scars.

"Perhaps," I replied. It was wise to be cautious. Time had already taught me that lesson.

"What?" he yelled.

I took a breath. "Perhaps!" I yelled back. The wind grew in ferocity. I suddenly realized the ridiculous nature of my circumstances, standing in a howling storm with a strange gentleman, yelling obscure answers into the rain. My gown was thoroughly soaked, hair plastered to my neck and cheeks, and my feet were glued to the mud. I was a sight, to be sure.

"I am going that direction as well. May I convey you and your maid to your destination?"

"Have you any females in your coach?" I asked.

"No." His eyes were dark against his shaded face. "Only a friend. But your maid will lend sufficient chaperonage."

I nodded, the rain making its way through every layer of clothing I wore and chilling my skin. If we did not get out of the rain right away, we were both bound to catch cold. "Lead the way, sir."

His elbow shot out, offering me an escort. I had been correct on that score, at least. He was a gentleman. I shook my head, lifting my skirts with both hands to keep them from the mud. He stood unmoving, his gaze trained on me as rain trailed down his cheeks and dripped from his straight nose.

I tried to step forward but struggled, my foot securely fastened to the mud. My balance thrown, my arms flailed, searching for purchase on the side of the slick carriage door.

Strong, cold hands came around my waist, catching me before I collided with the wet earth. Before I knew it, my legs flew into the air and I was bobbing forward. I wrapped my arms around the man's neck as he carried me around my carriage and to the doorway of his own. His heart pounded through his chest, the vibration chasing tingles down my side. I tightened my grip as the carriage door flew open, catching his eye suddenly. My cheeks warmed. He set my feet on the dry floor of his own cab and a man already seated inside reached forward to help me in.

I looked back over my shoulder and caught my stranger's stone face. Behind the mask, suppressed emotion begged release. Irritation, surely.

I moved aside to make room on the bench as my coachman ushered my maid in shortly behind me.

My toes squelched on the floor, my wet stockings sending a chill up my legs. I gasped, looking behind the man to the muddy road outside. "Sir, my shoes!"

"Are unquestionably useless," he countered, climbing inside to sit opposite me. He swung the door shut behind himself and hit the top of the carriage with his knuckles. When we failed to move, he did so again with more force, and the carriage slowly rolled forth.

"But what shall I wear?" I asked, looking behind me through the small window where my carriage sat in the mud, squat and unmoving like a sorrowful ruin. I saw my coachman climb inside to escape the rain while he waited with the carriage. It grew small in the distance then disappeared behind us. How was I going to pay for the repairs? How was I going to procure new *shoes*?

"You have only brought one pair?" he asked, one dark eyebrow arched up.

Affronted, I hardly knew what to say. "What business is that of yours?"

The men exchanged glances. Anger had caused my manners to slip and I felt a blush grow on my cheeks. I had not intended to sound so uncivil.

I would have been a simpleton not to notice that both of the men sitting opposite me were handsome, one as wet as I, the other completely dry. The dry man cleared his throat. "Perhaps we ought to introduce ourselves, given this unconventional situation. I am Mr. Andrew Peterson. This wet man is Lord Stallsbury."

Good gracious. A *lord*? And not just any lord, for his reputation preceded him. I swallowed. Being carried so intimately by a marquess known far and wide as a passionate gamester was not the correct way to guard my reputation.

They watched me expectantly and I squeezed my hands together in my lap. "A pleasure to meet you both, though I cannot say I am pleased with the circumstances. I am Mrs. Wheeler and this is my maid, Emma."

"I was unaware of a Mrs. Wheeler on the guest list," Mr. Peterson said to Lord Stallsbury. "Did Bancroft mention anything to you?"

Lord Stallsbury ran a hand over his face and through his hair, slicking water from it and spraying his friend. "I didn't ask. Though how would I when the correspondence was largely through you?"

"Excuse me," I interrupted. "Am I correct in assuming that you are traveling to Bancroft Hill on your own accord?"

"Yes," Lord Stallsbury said, the stone of his face replaced with slight irritation. I had heard many tales of his exploits in Town. If gambling did not take all of his money eventually, then drinking surely would. Word was, he was a scoundrel, and an imprudent one at that. "'Tis what I mentioned earlier."

"Oh." My conscience appeased, I relented. It appeared I was not putting them out very much at all. If one did not count the thoroughly wet bench seat and Lord Stallsbury's thoroughly wet person. But he was not the sort of man whose opinion I was overly concerned with. "And you are to attend the house party as well?"

"Yes," Lord Stallsbury confirmed.

I tried to ignore my warming cheeks. The man had only just carried me and now I was meant to attend a three-week-long house party with him. "If I may speak plainly, I would prefer it if the nature of my arrival in your carriage need not be repeated to the other guests. I can only imagine it would cause us undue discomfort."

Lord Stallsbury's searching gaze was guarded and I sallied forth. "Do not concern yourself with your actions for clearly they were necessary. I only mean that we ought to put it behind us so we might enjoy our stay at Bancroft Hill."

Silence reigned in the carriage. Perhaps the men were unused to such candor but I could not simply leave things unsaid. I did not regret my words.

Mr. Peterson said, "It shan't be much longer before we reach the house. I'd imagine a crew of men can fetch and repair your carriage on the morrow. The ferocity of these storms never lasts more than a day or so."

Nodding, I glanced at Emma. She sat quietly on the seat beside me, the fear on her face gone. It was likely replaced with the thrill of rescue by two handsome strangers. I could not help but feel like I would have enjoyed the adventure in my youngers years, as well. But of course, I'd had enough adventure in my young life to satisfy me. I did not need any more now than I was able to glean from my novels.

No, what I needed was a nice, steady man who could lend me his name, protection, and financial security. A staid man like Mr. Bancroft.

The Mr. Bancroft who I had once nearly rejected because of the very qualities that drew me toward him now. Though we had been separated before any rejection occurred; he was never given the opportunity to offer for me then.

Shivering, I wrapped my arms around my waist, but I could not keep my teeth from chattering.

"Take this," Lord Stallsbury said, handing me a folded blanket. He gave another to Emma and then wrapped a third around his own legs. He was visibly shivering as well, and guilt pierced me for arguing with him in the rain. If this powerful lord was to become ill due to my recklessness and broken carriage, then Mrs. Bancroft would surely not be pleased. If I remembered correctly, to make Mr. Bancroft happy, the happiness of his mother was paramount.

About the Author

Kasey Stockton is a staunch lover of all things romantic. She doesn't discriminate between genres and enjoys a wide variety of happily ever afters. Drawn to the Regency period at a young age when gifted a copy of *Sense and Sensibility* by her grandmother, Kasey initially began writing Regency romances. She has since written in a variety of genres, but all of her titles fall under clean romance. A native of northern California, she now resides in Texas with her own prince charming and their three children. When not reading, writing, or binge-watching chick flicks, she enjoys running, cutting hair, and anything chocolate.

Made in United States
North Haven, CT
16 July 2025

70750443R00152